"We're going to play a game. It's kind of an experiment, and very, very secret. Can you keep a secret?"

Davy nodded, happy and excited.

"Come over to the window seat with me. That's right. Now, sit very close." I put the beach bag over one shoulder and the other arm around Davy, spreading the travel folder across our laps. "Now, look at the picture, the big one in the center. We're going to look at it really hard, and we're going to imagine we're there, in that picture, and that picture is a real place."

"You mean we're going to pretend?"

"Right. We're going to pretend that we're on that beach, standing on this spot right here." I pointed to the sand under a palm tree. "Now we have to concentrate *very* hard. Ready?"

"Yup."

I stared at the travel folder, wishing myself back on Mirabelle Island. Believe it's real, I told myself. It's real and we're really there. Remember the bright sun, the splash of little waves, the warm air, the rippled sand. . . .

"Hey, where are we?" Davy shouted.

I blinked. We sat in shallow water, Davy still between my legs, the beach bag floating beside us.

"It worked," I whispered. "It really worked!"

THE · ANYWHERE · RING

MIRACLE ISLAND

Louise Ladd

BERKLEY BOOKS, NEW YORK

MIRACLE ISLAND

A Berkley Book / published by arrangement with
the author

PRINTING HISTORY
Berkley edition / July 1995

ISBN: 0-425-14879-3

BERKLEY®
Berkley Books are published by The Berkley Publishing Group,
200 Madison Avenue, New York, New York 10016.
BERKLEY and the "B" design
are trademarks belonging to Berkley Publishing Corporation.

PRINTED IN THE UNITED STATES OF AMERICA

10 9 8 7 6 5 4 3 2 1

For my agent, Mary Jack Wald,
who makes Miracles happen
and dreams come true.

MIRACLE ISLAND

chapter one

"I hate boys!" I shouted into the phone.

Carly chuckled. "Yeah, right." Her voice echoed because she was using her speakerphone.

"I mean it, Carly, I really hate them!" I banged the saltshaker on the kitchen table to emphasize my point.

"No, you don't. Just because one jerk pulled a mean trick on you doesn't—"

"How could I be so dumb, Carly? Why did I smell those flowers? *Why?*"

"Everyone smells flowers, Jenny. It's the normal thing to do."

I turned the saltshaker upside down and watched the tiny white grains pour out. "I should have known not to take those daisies from Darren. I should have guessed he'd pull a stupid trick like that."

"You thought—we *all* thought—he was congratulating you for making the basket that won the game."

"I should have known better. But no, I had to get all excited, with everyone watching. I even—ugh!—let him kiss my cheek!"

"Listen, Jenny, any girl would have been excited to get flowers from Darren. He *is* one of the cutest boys in school, even if he's also a total toad. Only Darren would think it's funny to sprinkle sneezing powder on flowers."

"I must have looked like such an idiot, sneezing like crazy, my face all red and blotchy. As if I weren't ugly enough already." I watched the salt form a miniature mountain.

"You're not the least bit ugly, and you know it. But it was a gross thing to do," Carly said.

"It was so awful, the whole school laughing at me, especially the boys."

"They weren't really laughing at you—"

"Yes, they were! And I hate every one of them. I'll never speak to a boy again!" I slammed down the shaker. "Ever!" I smashed my fist into the pile of salt.

Carly sighed. "They're not all jerks like Darren. Some of them are nice. Scott Daniels told me—"

"Scott Daniels!" I squeaked. He was *the* cutest boy in the entire seventh grade. I'd never spoken to him, not even a "hi" as we passed in the hall. Just the sight of him turned my knees to Jell-O. "Was he there?"

"Yes, and he said he felt sorry for you—"

"Sorry for me! Great! Just *great*!" I slumped over the kitchen table, too miserable to hold my head up. "My reputation is ruined forever. Not that I ever had one in the first place. Except as the klutziest girl in school."

"Jenny, you're not klutzy, you're just shy around boys."

I groaned again. She was right. "How do you do it, Carly? You talk to everyone, even the truly hunky guys, like they're real people."

"I just pretend they *are* real people."

"Ugh." The sleeve of my sweater was coated with salt. I tried to shake it off. "I don't ever want to see another male person as long as I live."

"Well," she said, "you're going to see a few of them at Bethany's Valentine's Day party."

"Oh no," I wailed. "I won't go!"

"Look, Jenny, it's not until five o'clock on Sunday and this is only Friday night. You've got practically the whole weekend to—"

"I can't! All those boys! And what if that jerk Darren is there?"

"What if he is? Just ignore him."

"How?" I began to draw designs in the salt scattered over the table. "But how can I skip it? Everyone will know why I didn't show up. They'll all be talking about me."

"Not if we think up a really good excuse," she said. When Carly and I needed to, we could come up with some truly awesome fibs.

Miss Cuddy pushed open the kitchen door and glared at me through her thick glasses. She reminded me of a skinny old owl. "It's almost your bedtime, Jennifer. I promised your parents I would see that you children went to sleep at proper hours. Say good night to your friend and hang up the phone."

"I'm allowed to stay up until eleven on weekends, Miss Cuddy," I said politely.

"Hmmph," she snorted. "Far too late, in my opinion." She crossed her arms. "What's that white stuff all over the table?"

"I, uh, spilled some salt. By accident."

"Well, clean it up, and please be quiet when you go upstairs. My favorite television program is starting in a few minutes."

I wanted to say, "*Every* TV show is your favorite, Miss Cuddy-couch-potato." I didn't say it. When you're thirteen there are lots of things you'd like to say to grown-ups, but don't. Not if you're smart.

Instead, I said, "I'll be quiet."

"And check on your brother." She pulled her ratty cardigan tighter across her bony chest. "I sent him to bed, but he's a stubborn child, and I'm not sure he followed instructions."

"Davy's a good kid!" I said, furious with her.

She sniffed. "He has yet to prove it to me!" She went out, leaving the kitchen door open.

I got up and closed it, then returned to the phone. "Carly, I don't know if I can stand one more day with that lady, and this is only Friday. Mom and Dad won't be back until Wednesday."

"Hang in there," Carly said. "This time next week she'll be history."

"If next week ever comes," I muttered. "I may not

make it through Sunday. Oh Carly, what am I going to do?"

"Go to the party. Just walk in like you're Princess Di and pretend you've never heard of Darren-the-weirdo."

"I wish I *looked* like Princess Di. That would make it easier."

"Jenny, stop dumping on yourself. You look great."

"No, I don't. I'm too tall."

"Jennifer Delaney! You have the world's worst inferiority complex! You should be glad you're not short like me, with a zillion freckles and red Brillo hair."

"But you're cute, Carly, everyone knows that. There's nothing special about me. I'm just so ordinary."

"Well, maybe you'll never be Miss America, but you've got a lot going for you."

"Like what?" I was begging for a compliment and Carly knew it, but hey, what are best friends for?

I could hear the smile in her voice. "Like nice long legs, and no zits. And unfrizzy hair. And you have beautiful eyes."

"I do?"

"Don't you ever look in the mirror?" She laughed. "Listen, I've got to go. I have to get up early—I'm baby-sitting for the Cranes all day. Let me know what you decide about the party. If you're not going, we'll need a little time to think up a really good excuse."

"Yeah, okay. Thanks. Good night, Carly." I hung up the phone and wiped off the table, then trudged up to my room and flopped down on the window seat, listening to the freezing rain hiss past my window.

If only Mom and Dad had taken me along on their vacation! I picked up the travel folder of Mirabelle Island and opened it. Glossy print gushed, *the ultimate holiday . . . balmy breezes . . . pristine beaches . . . romantic sunsets . . . dancing under the stars . . .*"

I desperately wanted to see this gorgeous, romantic island, and I desperately did *not* want to be in Clark Harbor, Connecticut, especially not on Sunday at five o'clock.

"Jen-neee, can I come in?" Davy thumped on the door.

"Go away! I'm studying!" I put my hand over the pictures, just in case he could see through the door with X-ray eyes.

"You're always studying," he complained.

"Go to bed, Davy, it's late."

"But—but—but—" Any second now he'd burst into tears.

I had to stop him fast. "Do you want to get Miss Cuddy up here?"

"No . . ." Davy's voice sank so low I could hardly hear him. "But, Jen-neee—"

"Go to bed! I'm busy!"

Silence. A minute later I heard his door close.

That was mean and I knew it. I felt terrible. Poor Davy. It wasn't his fault, but he was such a pain. He'd been hanging all over me since Mom and Dad left.

I twisted the garnet ring on my finger. It used to

belong to my great-grandmother and Mom had given it to me on my thirteenth birthday. It was a very special present, a family heirloom. I loved the beautiful filigree setting and the deep red stone, but I'd had it less than a week and I still wasn't used to wearing it.

Forget about Davy, I told myself. He should have been asleep by now. I had a right to be miserable all by myself, didn't I? Just because our parents went off and left us so they could have a second honeymoon, why did I have to become Davy's substitute mother? Just because he was only six years old? Just because he had no one else to help him?

I wondered if it was possible to feel any worse than I felt right that moment. If only I were on Mirabelle Island with Mom and Dad!

I looked at the travel folder again. The center picture showed a soft blue sky; the palm trees looked like they'd been made in Hollywood, and miles of white sand curved off into the distance. But it was the water that really got me, a sparkling color between blue and green, so clear I was dying to plunge in.

A sob came through the wall from Davy's room. I tried to concentrate on the picture. In the distance I could see foamy white spray where the waves hit the reef. . . .

Davy sobbed again, a terrible heartbroken sound. I jumped up and jerked my door open, then stopped in the hall and listened. The sound of canned laughter meant Miss Cuddy was glued to a sitcom. I tiptoed down the hall to Davy's room.

He lay facedown on the bed. How could I be so awful to my baby brother? I was turning into some kind of monster.

I sat down on the bed and pulled him onto my lap. He buried his wet face in my shirt. "Hey, Davy, it's okay. I'm sorry, really I am. Jenny's here now, everything's okay."

I went on talking until his sobs turned into hiccups. He drank a glass of water and I helped him into his pajamas, then sat beside him, patting his back, until he finally fell asleep.

Tucking the blankets tighter around him, I gave him an extra little pat and went out into the hall. I was mad at myself for being mean to Davy, and mad at Darren-the-jerk for making me be mean, and mad at Miss Cuddy for being Miss Cuddy. My parents should have known she was a dragon lady. They should have seen through all that fakey-sweetness in the interview.

My room was stuffy—the dragon kept the heat up so high I'd be roasted medium-rare by the time my parents got home. I opened the window partway. The fresh smell of rain and wind made me even madder. Stupid weatherman, I thought, taking off my clothes. Didn't he know it was supposed to *snow* in February?

I dug out my ancient Poochie the Puppy Dog pajamas. They were ragged and much too short, but the old flannel was as soft as a kitten's tummy and right then I needed a bit of comfort. I didn't care if I looked like a scarecrow, with my wrists and ankles sticking out way below the cuffs. For once it didn't matter that I was too tall, taller than most of the boys in my class. Mom says they'll catch up to me someday, but who can wait for someday?

If only I could be anyone else but me. And anywhere else but here. Picking up the travel folder, I took it over to the window seat. I studied the sunlit center picture again, playing with my ring. The water was so clear I could see the rippled sand underneath. I could almost feel myself wade into that silky water, the sand squishing between my toes, the tiny waves lapping my ankles, my knees, my waist, my shoulders. I floated, feeling the heat of the sun warming my face, the ocean lifting and falling gently, rocking me.

Slowly, slowly, I turned over and floated facedown, watching sunlight dance on the sand. Pale green seaweed drifted lazily past like hair ribbons in a summer breeze.

Slowly, slowly, I turned to face the sun again, feeling as loose and free as a gull on the wind. Time passed and time stood still and I floated, floated, floated . . . this is the way it should be, I thought, always and forever—

"Jennifer! Turn out your light!" Miss Cuddy pounded on the door. "It's past your bedtime!"

I opened my eyes and blinked as my room came into focus. My room. The cold rain. Miss Cuddy. "No, no," I mumbled. "Let me go back to sleep. . . . "

"What did you say?" Miss Cuddy opened the door. "Good grief, it's freezing in here. Why is that window open?" She marched across the room, reached past me, and slammed it shut.

I scrunched into the corner of the window seat as she glared down at me. "For heaven's sake, you're soaking wet!" She peered closer. "What's that?"

"Wh-what?"

She pointed. "There's something green in your hair."

I reached up and felt something slimy. I jerked it out and stared. It wasn't . . . no, it couldn't be . . .

Seaweed?

chapter two

I quickly closed my hand over the sea—uh, green thing—and looked around the room. Was I still dreaming? No, Miss Cuddy was real—too real—standing there in her frayed bathrobe, those sharp eyes demanding an answer.

"Um, um . . ." What could I say? "Uh . . . it—it must be a leaf. I was . . . I was leaning out the window. . . . " That had to be it, I thought.

"A leaf? A green leaf in February?" She sniffed.

I had to get rid of her. Fast. "Uh, Miss Cuddy, I—I don't feel well. M-maybe my cold is coming back." The dragon was terrified of germs. She almost refused to stay with us when she found out I'd been sick, but Mom convinced her I wasn't contagious any longer. Too bad.

"Not a relapse!" Miss Cuddy quickly moved toward the door. "It's no wonder, hanging out the window, getting soaking wet, staying up past your bedtime . . .

children today . . ." She opened the door. "Take two aspirin and go to bed. Good night." She left.

I opened my fist and stared at the sea—uh, thing. It was pale, shiny green. I poked it. It was slippery. It sure looked like . . . felt like . . . even smelled like seaweed.

But it couldn't be. The only way . . . but that was totally, absolutely impossible. *Totally, absolutely, completely impossible.*

I shivered and realized that Miss Cuddy was right: I was soaking wet. And covered with goose bumps. A hot shower was what I needed. A nice hot shower would clear my head of this weird dream. Because it had to be a dream, didn't it? Of course it did.

I grabbed my robe and tiptoed out into the hall. Downstairs, the eleven o'clock news was blasting out the problems of the world. Between the news and the late show, Miss Cuddy was safely out of the way for a while.

The steamy shower spray felt great. At first. Until I felt something gritty under my feet. I knelt down. Sand. There was sand in the bathtub. There wasn't any sand in the tub this morning. Feeling shaky, I checked between my toes. A few grains clung to my skin.

I stood up, closed my eyes, and let the water beat down on my head. I hadn't really walked into that sea, had I? Maybe I *was* getting sick again. Maybe I was running a fever and—I looked down at the tub again. Bits of green seaweed swirled around the drain.

This was just *too weird*. I turned off the water and snatched up the paper cup where I'd put the first piece of seaweed. It was still there: limp, but there.

I jammed it in my bathrobe pocket, dried off, and was almost out the door when I thought of the tub. Grabbing a washcloth, I wiped up each grain of sand, every tiny scrap of seaweed. Then I rinsed out the cloth until I was sure all traces of—Mirabelle Island?—were safely floating down the Connecticut sewer system.

In bed, snug under my quilt, I felt my forehead. If I had a fever, it wasn't much of one. Not enough to make me think I'd actually gone to— Stop it, Jen, I told myself. *It didn't happen.* I mean, how could it? How could I get . . . there . . . then back here? I couldn't. Everyone knows the world doesn't work that way.

Obviously, it was all just a dream. A nice dream, a fabulous dream, but it was *only* a dream. . . . I fell asleep remembering ribbons of seaweed . . . hot sun . . . soft air . . . warm water . . . peace. . . .

I woke up to snow. Cold snow and a warm face. Not just face. Warm feet and ankles. And hands and wrists. Not only warm, but slightly pink. The rest of me was winter-pale. I sat in bed and stared at the various parts of me. You can't get sunburned in a dream, can you?

"Jenny! It's snowing!" Davy burst into my room. I'd told him a million times to knock first, but did he listen? I smiled at him anyway. He looked happy for the first time in days.

"Yeah, I see it is." I tried to forget about my pink parts.

"Can we build a snowman?"

I got up and looked out the window. "Not yet, silly, there's only about an inch on the ground."

"Hurry up! Get dressed!" Davy bounced on my bed. "Hey, why's your face so red?"

"I'm just kind of warm. I know, let's open the window and catch snowflakes on our tongues, all right?"

"All riiight!" He flew to the window and pushed it up.

The temperature must have fallen twenty degrees overnight. Sticking my head out was like plunging into a freezer. The cold felt good on my warm cheeks.

We caught snowflakes until we were shivering, then Davy left and I got dressed, trying not to think about the dream. But it was like the little rubber ball attached to those wooden paddles with a long rubber band. The harder you hit it, the faster it comes back.

The dream should have faded, the way dreams are supposed to. But I remembered every bright, clear moment. I also remembered the sand between my toes, and the seaweed in my hair.

Stop it, Jen, I told myself. There couldn't have been any sand or seaweed.

My hand didn't listen to me. Before I knew it, I'd reached in my bathrobe pocket and pulled out the paper cup. Seaweed. Crisp, dry seaweed.

* * *

Davy chattered away while I forced down spoonfuls of oatmeal mush. I tried to listen to him and block out last night. Finally I shook my head. Shook it hard. I couldn't shake the crazy idea away. Had I really gone to Mirabelle Island?

Of course not! I probably leaned out the window, just like I told Miss Cuddy. Seaweed could have blown in with the rain. After all, Long Island Sound was only a few miles away and didn't *Ripley's Believe It or Not* have all kinds of stories about fish and frogs raining down in odd places?

So how did I get sand between my toes? Maybe it came from last summer. After all, I hated to vacuum my room. The sand could have stayed in the carpet all this time and I *had* been barefoot. . . . Yeah, that was it. Of course.

Miss Cuddy came into the kitchen with a basket of laundry. She liked to get the chores over early so she could spend the rest of the day with the TV.

"Jennifer." Miss Cuddy dropped the basket next to my chair. "Hasn't your mother told you not to put wet clothes in the hamper? Just look at these!" She held up my pajamas. "I refuse—" She broke off and peered at me. "Why is your face so pink?"

"Ummm . . . ah . . . it—it's kind of warm in here. . . ." I fanned my face with my hand.

"Nonsense! You look feverish." She took a step back. "You've definitely had a relapse!" she announced. "Finish your breakfast and go straight upstairs to bed!"

"But what about our snowman?" Davy wailed. "Me and Jenny—"

"Jennifer will not be building any snowmen today."

"But she promised—"

"That's enough, David. Any more fuss and you will not be allowed outside either." Miss Cuddy whisked the oatmeal out from under my nose, dropped the bowl in the sink, and ran scalding water in it. "Hmmph, germs all over the place, I suppose, and me with my sinuses . . . I'm not as young as I used to be, you know."

"It's not fair," Davy whined.

Miss Cuddy glared at him. "All right, young man, I warned you—"

"It's okay, Miss Cuddy," I said quickly. "He'll be good now, won't you, Davy?"

"But—but—but—"

"Hey, I've got a great idea!" I said. "How about if you build the snowman in the backyard, right under my window, so I can watch you? It'll be almost like having me there!"

"No, it won't."

"Come on!" I grabbed his hand and dragged him out of the kitchen. Trying to sound cheerful, I said, "We'll go up to my room and decide on the best spot to build the snowman."

"But I don't wanna do it all by myself."

"Hey, *look* at all that snow!" I pointed out the window. "You really want to go outside, don't you?"

He nodded.

"Are you going to let Miss Cuddy stop you?"

"Miss Cuddy is mean!" he burst out.

"Yeah, she kind of is," I whispered. "But we're not going to let her win, are we?"

"No way!"

"Right! You're going to build the best snowman in the whole wide world. We'll show Miss Cuddy!"

"Yeah, we'll show her!"

By the time I got Davy stuffed into his snowsuit, I had managed to forget about last night for at least ten minutes. But the moment the door closed behind him, the dream came flooding back.

I ran up to my room and plopped down on the window seat. Leaning my warm forehead against the cool glass, I watched Davy come around the corner of the house, his red jacket a bright spot in a white world.

Davy waved and I waved back. He made a snowball, then began to roll it across the ground, packing extra snow on as he went. The flakes were coming down thick and fast, but the ground was barely covered. It was going to take a while to build a halfway-decent snowman.

Bits and pieces of the dream kept flashing in my mind. The feel of the silky warm water, the scent of the rich air . . . Cut it out, Jen. Think about something else.

Carly! I'll call Carly! I stood up but then remembered that she was baby-sitting for the Crane kids all day. I'd have to wait until she got through at five o'clock. Talking to her at that house was like trying to swim through a hurricane.

I paced around my room. Picked up a library book and put it down. Thought about doing some homework, but I never open my backpack until Sunday night; it's a matter of principle with me. Then I saw the invitation to Bethany's Valentine party on my bureau.

I couldn't believe that I hadn't thought about the party once this morning. Not since I went to—I mean, I had that dream about Mirabelle. Think about the party, Jen, it will take your mind off what you don't want to think about. Now, should you go or not?

What if Darren is there? How will I face him? But what if I don't go and he gets the guys together and they start laughing about me . . . ?

I couldn't win, no matter what I decided. I turned the invitation facedown and wandered over to my desk. The travel folder stared up at me. It felt like a magnet, pulling me, daring me. I fought for a moment but finally gave in and snatched it up. I opened it to the center picture and, for just a second, I could have sworn I'd been on that island. The feeling vanished and I saw an absolutely ordinary, glossy ad. I sailed it across the room and it landed on the window seat.

The darned thing wasn't going to leave me alone. I sighed and sat down with it.

I looked at the center picture again, idly playing with my ring. The feeling came back, stronger this time: I had been on that island. I had floated in that water, rocked by those tiny waves. I could feel the soft air, and the heat of the sun. The sun was so hot. It beat down on me, pounding through my clothes. A palm tree threw shadows across the beach. Under it, the sand was smooth and cool. I sank down and leaned back against the trunk, my eyes closed against the bright sparkle of the water. A breeze rustled the fronds overhead and brushed my hot face. I heard the slap of small waves and the distant buzzing of an insect.

"I suppose you're trying to avoid a sunburn," a voice said, "but that outfit is rather impractical, don't you think?"

My eyes popped open. A boy stood over me, wearing only a brief bathing suit and a tan.

"Wh-what?" I stammered.

He grinned and pointed to my clothes. "Jeans and a sweater are all very well up north, but aren't you rather warm in them down here?"

chapter three

"Wh-wh-wh-warm?" I stuttered. I'd almost said, "Where's here?" but one glance at the palm trees, the water, the sand told me I had to be on Mirabelle Island.

How did I get here?

"Yes, warm," the boy said, grinning. He spoke with a stuffy-sounding accent. "I gather you're new. Just arrived today, have you?"

"Y-yes." My mind was whirling.

"Been in the water yet?" He squatted down beside me.

"Yes. Earlier." Well, that was true, wasn't it? I'd been here last night, hadn't I? At least, if I was here now, I must have been here last night. But night at home was daylight on the island. I was getting more confused every second.

"I say, you really look awfully warm." He had

dark brown eyes, ears that stood out like an elephant's, and a grin that lit up his entire face.

"Well . . . I am a little warm. . . . " (I was *suffocating*!)

"Why don't you trot up to your cottage and change into your bathing suit? We can go for a swim."

My turtleneck was choking me. My wool sweater prickled with a thousand needles. I wanted to rip off these awful clothes and plunge into the water.

He was watching me. I must look totally ridiculous. Why did it have to be a *boy* who caught me in this horrible mess? "A swim?" I managed to say. "Th-that would be nice."

Only I didn't have a cottage to "trot up to" and my bathing suit was back in Clark Harbor. I'd have to fake it. I couldn't stay here anyway.

I scrambled to my feet and he stood up too. He was several inches taller, with a swimmer's slim body and wide shoulders. He was probably about my age, but his accent made him sound older.

I looked around. Where the heck was "my cottage" supposed to be? The beach was bordered with a strip of grass and a hedge of thick bushy plants dotted with pink flowers. A sandy path led through the bushes and, in the distance, I saw several red-tiled roofs.

"Are you in Hibiscus, Bougainvillea, or Gardenia?" he asked.

"What?"

"Your cottage. Which group are you in?"

"Um, Hibiscus, I guess," I mumbled. He must

think I'm *so weird.* "I—I'm sorry, I uh, just got here and it's all so . . . new."

"I was a bit confused myself at first. Jet lag, you know. Takes several days to accustom oneself to the time difference." He looked at his watch. "Right now it's dinnertime in London."

"Is that where you're from, London?" I asked. That's why his accent was kind of stuffy—he was English.

"Yes, where are you from?"

"Connecticut. That's in the United States."

"Really? I thought it was in Russia." His grin flashed again.

I blushed. I'd better get out of here before I made an even bigger fool of myself. If that was possible.

"Well, I'll go . . . change." I started toward the path.

"Wait a moment," he called after me.

Now what? Was I going the wrong way to Hibiscus? If I was, I didn't want to know about it. I kept walking.

"I say, wait," he called again.

I stopped and turned around. He shouted, "What's your name?"

Was that all? I went limp with relief. "Jenny!" I yelled.

"I'm Stephen!"

I nodded, waved, and hurried to the path. Once I was safely in the bushes, I looked back. He was already in the water, swimming out toward the reef.

What would he think when I didn't return? Forget

it, Jen, I told myself. Even if he does have a cute smile, he's just a stranger and you'll never see him again. Besides, you're through with boys forever. You hate them, remember?

That water sure looks fabulous, though, I thought. Next time I'll wear my bathing suit. Hey, what next time? Never mind coming back! How the heck did I get here? And how was I going to get home?

I was so *hot.* Sweat trickled down my forehead and my turtleneck clung to me like plaster. I was about to pull off my sweater when I glimpsed two people coming down the path. I did *not* want to meet anyone else. No way. I dove headfirst into the bushes, pushing through the stiff branches until I found a spot big enough to crouch in.

I heard a male voice as they came nearer. "Let's skip the disco tonight, all right? My back will never be the same again."

"What, and admit we're old fogies who can't keep up with the kids?" the woman teased.

It was Mom and Dad! My very own parents and I'd almost run into them! What if I had? How would I ever explain how I got here? Talk about close calls. . . .

THUNK! A snowball smashed into the window by my head. Shocked, I jumped up and almost fell. I was dizzy and my heart pounded like a rock band. I sat back down and my room came into focus. My room. I was back in Clark Harbor.

Another snowball exploded on the window and

slithered down the glass. I opened the window and yelled, "Davy! Stop that! You're going to break something!"

Davy looked up at me. "But you didn't answer! I called and called and you never answered me! You said you'd help me!"

I shook my head, more confused than ever. Was I cracking up? First I think I'm on Mirabelle Island, talking to a boy named Stephen, and almost running into Mom and Dad, and then I'm back in Connecticut, which I never left anyway . . . I automatically brushed the sand from the seat of my pants.

And froze. Stared at the white grains of sand on my carpet.

"Jen-neee! Answer me!" Davy shouted.

I made myself look out the window. "What did you say, Davy?"

"I *said,* is the snowman big enough yet?" He pointed to a smallish mound.

"N-no, not yet, Davy. You can make it lots bigger."

"But I've used up all the snow."

Brown grass showed in a ragged circle around the snowman.

"Get some from the driveway," I said.

"How?"

"Use the snow shovel!" I slammed my window down.

Be cool, Jen, be cool, I told myself over and over. I took a deep breath and tried to think.

I felt my turtleneck. It was damp with sweat. Bits of leaves and torn pink petals clung to my sweater.

My eyes kept going back to the white sand on the floor.

It was totally impossible. And it was totally real. The sand was real. The leaves and petals and sweat were real. If you put all the facts together, it sure as heck looked like I'd just been to Mirabelle Island. It couldn't be true . . . but it *had* to be true.

Once before I'd felt something turn over inside me, so that what I believed was suddenly *not* what I believed. That was when I found out about Santa Claus. And now it happened again. It finally hit me that I had really, truly gone to Mirabelle Island. And come back again.

I let out a whoop of joy. "I did it! I did it! I did it!"

I danced around the room a bit, then suddenly stopped. More than anything I'd ever wanted before, I wanted to go back again. But how?

chapter four

The attic was dusty and freezing cold. It took a while to find the box with my bathing suit. I didn't know if I could go back to Mirabelle Island, but if I did, I was sure as heck going *prepared.* I found my suit and grabbed my long flamingo T-shirt to wear over it. Then I came across Davy's suit. I held it up and thought, Should I take him along? *Could* I take him along?

Why not? At least I could try. He'd love the island. Also, who-knows-what might happen if I left him alone with Miss Cuddy. If my experiment didn't work, I'd just tell Davy it was a silly old game. He'd believe me.

By the time I found the beach towels and suntan lotion and a plastic zipper bag, lunch was ready. The dragon made me eat alone in my room so I wouldn't spread my "germs" around, but I whispered to Davy, telling him to sneak upstairs as soon as he could.

At 12:30 Davy burst into my room. "She's watching some old movie on TV," he reported. "Hey, how come you're wearing your bathing suit?"

"We're going to play a game. It's kind of an experiment, and very, very secret. Can you keep a secret?"

He nodded, happy and excited.

"Okay," I said. "Now this game may not work, but even if it doesn't, it's still a secret. Promise you won't tell *anyone*?"

He nodded again. "Sure."

"I mean *no one.* Not *ever.* Do you promise?"

"I *said* yes."

"Cross your heart and hope to die?"

"Cross my heart and hope to die. So why are you wearing your bathing suit?"

"You'll see. *If* it works." I handed him his suit and a T-shirt. "Go put these on."

"Why?"

"Don't ask questions. I told you, you'll see."

He left, and while he was gone I glanced at myself in the mirror, then sighed. A raving beauty I was definitely not. If I should happen to run into that English guy, Stephen, again . . . My heart beat a little faster for a moment. He wasn't exactly handsome, but when he smiled . . . Forget it, Jen, I told myself, he's a boy, a person of the male species, and they're nothing but trouble. Period. I put on my flamingo shirt and rechecked the plastic beach bag.

"I'm ready!" Davy ran into the room. "Now what? Are we going swimming?"

"Maybe, if the experiment works." I locked the

door. "But remember, it might not work—it probably won't—so don't be too disappointed."

"How can I be disappointed when I don't know what to be disappointed *about*?"

I laughed. "Come over to the window seat with me. That's right. Now, sit very close." I put the beach bag over one shoulder and the other arm around Davy, spreading the travel folder across our laps. "Now, look at the picture, the big one in the center. We're going to look at it really hard, and we're going to imagine we're there, in that picture, and that the picture is a real place."

"You mean we're going to pretend?"

"Right. We're going to pretend that we're on that beach, standing on this spot right here." I pointed to the sand under a palm tree. "Now, we have to concentrate *very* hard. Ready?"

"Yup."

It was the best I could do. I'd tried to remember exactly how it happened the first two times and this is what I came up with. I stared at the travel folder, wishing myself back on Mirabelle Island. Believe it's real, I told myself. It's real and we're really there.

Nothing happened. I glanced at Davy. He was looking at the picture, his eyes enormous. It wasn't his fault. He was trying.

Maybe it wouldn't work with two people. But that didn't make sense. If one could do it, why not two?

I went back to studying the picture. It had happened twice. It had to happen again, didn't it? What was I forgetting? What did I do before that was different? Nothing. I'd just been looking at the picture, thinking myself there and *zap!* I was on the island. I had to try harder, concentrate harder—

"Ouch," Davy pulled his arm away from my hand. "Your ring's digging me."

I saw the red mark on his arm where I'd been holding him. An outline of my ring. My ring! Wasn't I playing with it the other times? Yes, I was, twisting it around, sliding it up and down my finger.

"Maybe that's it!" I said out loud.

"What's it?" Davy asked.

"Let's try something different. Move over here and sit between my legs. That way I can put both arms around you," and play with my ring, I added silently.

We rearranged ourselves, but still nothing happened. I was too conscious of the ring, trying to remember exactly what I'd done. Stop thinking, Jen. Concentrate on Mirabelle Island. Remember the bright sun, the splash of little waves, the warm air, the rippled sand. . . .

"Hey, where are we?" Davy shouted.

I blinked. We sat in shallow water, Davy still between my legs, the beach bag floating beside us.

"It worked," I whispered. "It really worked!"

"Where *are* we?" Davy stood up.

"Mirabelle Island!" I jumped up. "It *worked*!"

"You mean we're really here? We're not pretending?"

"We're really here!" I waded ashore, so pleased with myself I could hardly stand it.

"Wow!" Davy slapped the water. "Wow! This is neat! This is super-super neat!"

I looked around. "Yeah, it sure is."

"Where'd you say we are? Miracle Island?"

I laughed. "That's it, all right. This really is a miracle island."

"How'd we get here?"

"I'm not sure. It's some kind of magic, I guess." I touched the garnet ring, my "eccentric" great-grandmother's ring. I didn't remember her, but my mother used to tell us stories: how she would lock herself in her room for hours at a time and only her maid was allowed to enter her room when she had one of her "headaches." And how, after a headache, foreign words and phrases would pop into her conversation and everyone would have to pretend they hadn't heard. And how she loved to surprise the family with presents like ivory fans and silk scarves and llama rugs.

I smiled. I had an idea I knew what caused all those "headaches."

Suddenly I remembered the letter. It came with the ring, but I hadn't bothered to read all of it yet. My great-grandmother's handwriting was spidery and faded, hard to make out. The part I'd read just told why I'd inherited the ring and said to take good care of it. Why didn't I finish the letter? How dumb could I be?

"Come on, Jenny, come in the water with me. I want to swim." Davy tugged at his T-shirt.

"Wait a second, we have to put on suntan lotion

first. We can't get burned." I promised myself I'd read the whole letter the first chance I got. But now I had figured out how to bring us to Miracle Island and I was going to enjoy every second of it.

I dug around in the beach bag until I found the bottle of lotion. It was rated number twelve and I hoped it would be strong enough. I sure didn't want to explain a sunburned Davy to Miss Cuddy in Connecticut.

"Is that how your face got so pink?" Davy asked as I slathered lotion on him. "You were here before?"

I nodded. For a little kid, Davy was pretty smart sometimes.

"Hurry *up*!" He squirmed under my hands. "I want to go swimming!"

I smoothed the lotion down the back of his legs and let him go. He scampered into the water.

I rubbed lotion on my own legs, arms, and face. The air was heavy and warm, even though the sun was pretty low in the sky now. I couldn't wait to plunge in.

"If you'll take off that nightshirt, I'll do your back for you," a male voice said.

I whipped around. The boy—Stephen—stood there, grinning at me.

He said, "I don't usually take kindly to being stood up, but I imagine in your case, you have a perfectly good explanation."

"Umm, y-y-yes. Sure." Why was my heart pounding so hard?

"Yes, I thought so. Would you care to share it with me—the explanation, I mean?"

"Ummm, ah . . . ummm, my—my brother!" I pointed to Davy, splashing and whooping in the shallows. "I, uh . . . had to take care of him."

"And I suppose your parents wouldn't allow you to bring him down to the beach, of course."

"Of course," I repeated. "I mean, uh, Davy didn't—didn't want to come to the beach. He wanted to . . . ah . . ."

"Swim in the pool, perhaps?" Stephen suggested.

"Yes, that's right! He wanted to go to the pool!" I smiled with relief.

He gave me a funny look but said, "Come on, take off that shirt so I can do your back. You do want to go for a swim, don't you?"

"Uh, yeah." I peeled off my flamingo shirt and turned around, wondering why I was letting this guy do this.

I jumped at the cold shock of lotion on my back.

"You do realize," he said as he worked the lotion up my neck, "this will wash off in the water?"

"Yes, but it's better than nothing. It was all I could find and if Miss Cuddy—" I bit my lip.

"Who is Miss Cuddy?"

"No one! I mean, she's just this old dragon who . . . who . . ." Change the subject, Jen. Quickly. Say something. Say *anything.* I looked around. "Where—where is everyone?" Unlike last time, only a few people were scattered around, down at the other end of the beach.

"Cocktail time for the adults, teatime for the kiddies. It's after five, you know."

"Oh. Yes. Right." Keep your mouth shut, Jen. Everything you say gets you in deeper.

Stephen turned me around to face him. "Look, Jenny, you can trust me. I know we've only met briefly, but I'm terribly curious, and I won't say a word to anyone. Ever since I saw you appear from nowhere in those ridiculous pajamas—"

Pajamas? I screamed silently. *He saw me the first time in my little-girl Poochie the Puppy Dog pajamas?*

"Jen-neee!" A small wet head butted me in the stomach. "Are you coming swimming or *what*?"

"Yes!" I ran across the sand, dived in, and swam out to sea.

chapter five

I swam and swam, but I couldn't get away from the picture in my mind. Stephen watching me floating in the ocean in my raggedy old pajamas. My Poochie the Puppy Dog pajamas!

He must have laughed his head off. Why did God ever invent boys in the first place? They were all the same—they just wanted to make girls feel ridiculous. Stephen was probably laughing at me right now. I groaned out loud. The only thing to do was to keep swimming until I hit Australia.

Except my arms and legs didn't cooperate. They got heavier and heavier and my breath came faster and faster. Finally I couldn't lift one more arm, or give one more kick. Groaning again, I rolled over on my back and floated.

That's when I realized my pajamas weren't the only problem. Stephen had seen me appear out of nowhere. And how was I going to explain *that*?

How do you explain the impossible?

You can't.

Okay, Jen, I told myself, so don't. You don't have to explain *anything* to Stephen. You don't even have to see him again. You can stay right here, floating in the middle of the ocean until the magic zaps you back to Clark Harbor.

And leave Davy here? I groaned again. I was getting good at groaning. I sounded like a pregnant whale.

What would Miss Cuddy say if she found out I'd left Davy on a Caribbean island? What would *Mom and Dad* say?

This magic business sure had a way of complicating life.

I rolled over and started slowly back to shore, my tired muscles swearing at me with each stroke. Suddenly something grabbed my ankle and dragged me underwater. Totally panicked, I opened my eyes and saw Stephen blowing bubbles at me. Furious, I kicked to the surface.

"You scared me to death!" I yelled the moment his head popped up.

"Sorry." He didn't look sorry at all. "Your brother asked me to fetch you. He wants you to play with him."

"He *always* wants me to play with him." I was so mad I forgot to be embarrassed. "Why don't *you* play with him instead?"

"Why don't we both?" He had a lot of nerve, flashing that grin at me. "Come on, I'll race you."

He took off and I followed slowly. By the time I caught up, Stephen was in waist-deep water, trying to get Davy to climb on his shoulders.

"Come on, old chap, it's easy. Just grab my hands," Stephen said.

Davy looked at me, worried. "Can I, Jenny?"

"Sure. Why not?" If Stephen kept busy with Davy, maybe he'd forget about me.

Davy looked suspicious. "We're not supposed to talk to strangers," he recited.

"He's not a stranger, he's Stephen."

"Did you meet him when you came before?"

"Uh . . . yes." I frowned. "I met him when I *came down to the beach* before." Did he get my warning? "Go on, see what happens."

Stephen squatted down in the water and showed Davy how to balance his feet on those broad shoulders. Then, big hands gripping little ones, they stood up. "Ready?" Stephen asked. "All right, one, two, three, *go*!"

Davy jumped and landed in a belly flop, but he scrambled right back onto Stephen's shoulders. One belly flop followed another until finally Davy made a perfect dive and we clapped.

"It's time for tag!" Stephen announced. He tapped my arm. "Jenny, you're it!"

He and Davy began to swim away and I stood there, hesitating. True, Stephen was a boy, and true, he was probably laughing at me, but I'd come to Miracle Island to have fun, didn't I? Was I going to let this guy spoil it? No way.

I splashed after the boys, and pretty soon I forgot everything but the game. I felt like a kid again; worries slid away. When we stopped to catch our breaths, I showed off with underwater handstands and somersaults. Davy wanted to dive again and Stephen talked me into trying it too, but each time he stood up I came crashing down like a Leaning Tower of Pizza.

It felt like just a short time later that I exploded to the surface after losing an underwater race. I stood up, breathing hard, and noticed that the sun was almost touching the ocean. Long shadows from the palm trees stretched across the sand. Several couples strolled along the beach. I blinked my salt-stung eyes. One couple looked *much* too familiar.

"Oh no, Mom and Dad!" I whispered.

"Jen-neee, look at me!" Davy stood on Stephen's shoulders, every inch of him visible from shore.

"Jump!" I ordered.

"What?"

No time to explain. I lunged at Stephen and shoved him—hard. Davy flew into the water.

He popped up like a cork. "Hey, whatcha do that for?"

"Shhhh!" I glanced at the beach. My parents had stopped and were looking out at the water. Right at us. "Be quiet, do you hear? It's Mom and Dad."

"Really?" He started to wave.

I grabbed his arm. "You dumbbell! We can't let them see us! *Dive!*"

"Why?"

"Don't argue! Just *do it*!" I gave him half a second to take a breath, then pushed him under. Mom and Dad were shading their eyes, trying to see against the glare of the sun. I gulped air and sank under the water.

I stayed down forever. Just when I thought I was going to burst, a hand pulled me up. I surfaced, gasping like a fish on the dock.

"It's all right," Stephen said. "They've moved on." His back was toward the beach and he held Davy in front, shielding him with his body.

My parents were walking away, Mom's hands going a mile a minute, so I knew she was excited. But they couldn't have recognized us or Dad would have plunged into the water—slacks, shoes and all. I shivered with relief, watching until they were out of sight.

"Come along," Stephen said. "I think it's time we all took a rest, don't you?" I nodded and helped him herd a protesting Davy out of the water.

We found our towels and I insisted we move up near the bushes before we sat down. I knew Mom and Dad could return any minute and I sure as heck didn't want to be caught out in the open.

Davy, dripping wet and coated with sand, plunked himself down on the coarse sea grass. "Jenny, why couldn't we say hi to Mommy and Daddy?"

"Davy, you *know* why." I stopped toweling my hair and glared at him. "Remember? You *promised*."

"Oh. Yeah. It's a secret, right?"

"I don't understand," Stephen said. "You're not allowed to come to the beach?"

"No, *here*. Miracle Island," Davy said before I could stop him.

"You mean Mirabelle Island?" Stephen was puzzled.

"That's what Davy calls it—" I began.

"Yeah," Davy said. "Because we got here by magic."

"Davy!" I turned to Stephen, desperate. "He—he thinks it's magic because . . . because he's never flown on a plane before." I pushed out a little laugh. "You have to admit, it seems like magic, the way those huge things fly through the air."

"I quite agree," Stephen said. "It doesn't seem physically possible, does it?"

I relaxed a bit. "Mr. Bomberg explained it in science—"

"But, Jenny," Davy interrupted. "We didn't come on a plane—"

"David DeMatta Delaney!" I exploded. "Don't you dare say one more word!"

He scrunched up his face, then sighed. "You're so bossy." He plucked a blade of grass. "I'm hungry. Do they sell hamburgers here?"

Stephen started to answer, but I cut him off. "We'll eat later." Money! I forgot to bring money. Have to remember next time. I spread out my towel, sat down next to Davy, and put my arm around him. "Hey, didn't we have a good time? Wasn't the water fun?"

"Yeah, super!" He looked up at me, eyes shining. "Can we come back soon?"

"Sure. We can come *back to the beach* tomorrow." My warning frown was wasted. He was looking out to sea, where the sunset was turning the wispy clouds gold and lavender.

Stephen sat down beside me, his knee casually touching mine. Funny how that one little touch made me feel kind of tingly. "Jenny," he said quietly, "do you remember that I said you could trust me? You can, you know. I can be most discreet. Something very odd is happening, and I must admit I'm terribly curious. Won't you tell me?"

I glanced at him, then looked back at the sunset. In spite of being a boy, he was sort of nice. He'd even helped hide Davy from my parents, although it must have seemed strange to him that I was afraid of Mom and Dad. But there was no way I could tell him the truth. Even if I tried to explain it, he'd never believe—

Knock, knock, knock. "Jennifer, are you awake? It's Miss Cuddy. I've brought you some chicken soup." *Knock, knock*. "Jennifer, do you hear me?"

I stared at my room, shocked. My arm was still around a salty, sandy Davy. But worse, much worse, my knee was still touching a very tan, almost nude, totally bewildered Stephen.

chapter six

"I say, *what*—" Stephen began.

I clamped my hand over his mouth. "Shhhh! She'll hear you." In a louder voice I called, "Just a minute, Miss Cuddy, I'm getting dressed!"

I jumped up, dragging Davy with me. "But, Jenny, I don't want to come back! I want—"

"Not now, Davy. Quick, get in the closet!"

"Why?"

"Just hush up and do what I tell you." I gave him a push, then grabbed Stephen. "You too! *Now!* I'll explain later."

Stephen was too boggled to argue. I shoved him in the closet with Davy, threw the beach towels after them, grabbed my robe, and slammed the door shut.

Wrapping the robe over my bathing suit, I ran to the bedroom door and unlocked it. Miss Cuddy stood in the hall, holding a tray with a bowl of soup and a plate of crackers. "I'm sorry, Miss Cuddy, I just got out of the shower and I was getting dressed. . . . "

She pushed past me into the room, looking like she expected to find Dracula. "What was all that noise? Why are you so out of breath?"

"Uh, I was just hurrying . . . I didn't want to keep you waiting. . . . "

She put the tray down on my desk. "I'm sure I heard David's voice. What was he doing in your room while you were getting dressed? And where is he now?"

"D-Davy? He—he's not here. He . . . I was talking to him from my window. He's outside, playing in the snow."

Miss Cuddy marched over to my window and looked down, clutching her cardigan across her chest. "I don't see him."

"Oh? He—he must have gone around front." I walked over to the desk. "Thank you for the soup."

"Nothing like chicken soup for a cold." She peered at me. "Your face is redder than before. I'd better take your temperature."

"Oh no, that's okay, I feel great, really. It's just the . . . uh . . . heat from the shower."

She snorted. "Young people today. I've never heard of so many showers. How your parents can afford the hot water bill, I don't know. When I was your age—"

I faked a cough. "Um, Miss Cuddy, it was very nice of you to bring me the soup. I really appreciate it, but I don't want to expose you to my germs."

Miss Cuddy practically jumped at the mention of

germs. She moved quickly toward the door. "Eat your soup. And for heaven's sake, dry your hair. A wet head is the worst thing in the world for a cold, don't you know that?"

"Yes, Miss Cuddy."

"Children today," she muttered as she went out, slamming the door.

I collapsed on my bed and listened to her footsteps going downstairs.

The closet door opened a crack. "Is it safe to come out now?" Stephen whispered.

"Yes."

Davy burst out of the closet, furious. "Why'd you shut us in?"

I giggled. He looked so ridiculous standing there, his hair sticking out in all directions, still spotty with sand.

Stephen walked over to the window. "It's *snowing*! Where are we? What happened?"

Davy answered. "We're in Connecticut, at our house. We came by magic, like I told you."

Stephen said nothing, just looked at Davy, then back at the snow. His face went blank, like he'd pulled down a shade.

My giggles died away. Poor Stephen. "Don't worry, I'll take you back right away. It was a mistake. I think you came along with us because you were touching me when it happened."

"When *what* happened?" He dropped down on the window seat as if his legs had given out.

"When Miss Cuddy called me. See, I can control

the *going,* but not the coming back."

He shivered. "What *are* you *talking* about?"

"Davy," I said. "Run and get Dad's bathrobe, the big warm one."

"Aren't we going back to Miracle Island?" Davy was shivering too.

"Not yet. I have to figure something out first. Bring us the bathrobe, then go hop in the shower. And don't let Miss Cuddy catch you all covered with sand."

Davy went, protesting, but he went. He was back in a minute with the bathrobe, then, still complaining, left to take a shower.

"Jenny, would you *please* tell me what's going on?" The white robe set off Stephen's dark tan.

"It's a long story. Don't you want to go back to the island right away? But first, I have to figure out how to get home when I want to."

"What *are* you talking about?" he almost shouted.

I couldn't blame him. If I were in his place, I'd want to know too. He might be a boy, but I was beginning to think he was really a decent person and I owed him an explanation. Maybe now that he was caught in the impossible, it would be easier for him to understand.

I told him everything that had happened since Friday night. Except that I didn't mention my ring. Until I had a chance to read my great-grandmother's letter, I thought I'd better be smart and keep quiet about it.

I began with the first trip, skipping the part about my little-girl pajamas and hoping he wouldn't remember, and then described the others. At first he asked a million questions, but by the time I finished, he was quiet. He looked around my room, then out the window again, and finally said very slowly, "This really happened, didn't it?"

"Yup. I know it's hard to believe, but you really are in Connecticut."

"Yes, I can see that."

"And I really was on Miracle Island, wasn't I?"

"Yes, you were." He frowned, his funny face serious. I thought he'd already asked and I'd already answered every question in the world, but he said, "There's something odd I don't understand."

What could be odder than what I'd just told him?

"Jenny, you said it was nighttime when you, er . . . appeared on the island the first time. But it was late morning for me."

"What day of the week was it?" I asked.

"Saturday. Today."

"It's Saturday for me too, now. Only last night it was Friday."

He shook his head. "The second time, when you showed up in your winter clothes, it was only a few hours later, midafternoon, and this time, when you brought Davy, it was near sunset. But it's daytime here in Connecticut."

"I don't understand the time thing. It doesn't make sense."

"*None* of it makes sense, actually." He grinned for the first time since we'd arrived in Connecticut. "Are you sure you have absolutely no idea what makes this—magic—business happen?"

"Nope," I lied. I didn't want to, but I had to.

"Yet you're confident you can return me to Mirabelle?"

"Sure. The problem is, I don't know how I'll get home after I drop you off." I laughed. It sounded like I was offering to take him across town to the bus station.

He frowned. "What's so funny?"

"Uh, nothing." He was right; we were in deep trouble and it wasn't funny. If Stephen stayed much longer, Miss Cuddy would be sure to find him . . . the thought made me shudder. I had to take Stephen back, and soon.

I picked up the travel poster. How did I get home to Connecticut before? Last night Miss Cuddy woke me up from what I thought was a dream, this morning Davy threw a snowball at the window, and this last time Miss Cuddy brought me chicken soup.

Click! Each time, someone had been calling my name! "I've got it! I'll bet I've got it, Stephen!"

"Got what?" He looked absolutely miserable, huddled in Dad's bathrobe, watching the snow fall outside the window.

I quickly told him my theory.

"That sounds possible," he said. "But does it always work? Are you sure?"

"How can I be sure? There's only one way to find out. When I take you back to Miracle, Davy will have to stay behind and call me back."

"Are you willing to take the risk?"

"We don't have any choice," I said. "I've got to get you back to the island! We have to try it."

"Will Davy cooperate?"

I groaned. Davy would not be thrilled.

He wasn't. My little brother refused to let us go back to the island without him. I tried to reason with him, then I tried bribery. Nothing worked.

Finally I exploded. "David Delaney, you listen to me! I took you to Miracle, didn't I?"

He nodded.

"And you had a terrific time, didn't you?"

Another nod.

"And now I want you to do me one little favor. I need you to help me take Stephen back, and *you are going to help whether you like it or not*!"

He studied his toes. "Ummm, well, okay."

I shook my head. Why hadn't I just said that in the first place? Little brothers!

"Very good, Jenny," Stephen said with a small smile. "Now that Davy has so generously agreed to help, are you ready to leave?"

"Sure." I crossed my fingers, hoping my idea was right. If I got stuck on the island and left Davy alone here . . . what would he tell Miss Cuddy? What would *she* tell our parents?

I pushed the thought out of my mind. "Now, Davy, I'm going to set the alarm clock. When it goes off, you call me. Stand right here and say my name. Keep calling if you have to, but don't let Miss Cuddy hear you."

"Set it for two minutes," he demanded. "You have

to come back in *two minutes.*"

"Ten," I offered. We compromised on five.

Stephen and I took off our robes; I set the alarm and hurried over to the window seat next to Stephen, his arm on mine. I was surprised by that little tingly feeling again.

"Should we hold hands?" Stephen asked.

"Ummm, not this time . . ." We spread out the travel folder and I concentrated, playing with the ring.

We floated about fifty yards from shore, blinking in the glare of Miracle Island. The sun overhead turned each ripple of water into diamonds of light dancing in our eyes.

"Sunglasses," I muttered, treading water. "Remind me to bring sunglasses next time."

"I don't believe it," Stephen said. "It works! We're here!"

"Of course." I was rather proud of myself.

"I didn't feel a thing." He sounded a little stunned. "Wouldn't you think there should be some reaction—nausea or dizziness perhaps?"

"I felt dizzy once," I said. "But I think it was because I was so hot in my winter clothes. And worried about running into Mom and Dad."

"I can't believe it! This is incredible!" He slapped the water.

I looked around. Something wasn't right. *Something* was different from the way it should be, but I couldn't figure it out. "I guess we should say good-bye. Davy could call me anytime. He probably won't wait for the alarm. That is, *if* he can call me back."

"Fingers crossed." He grinned, then glanced toward shore. "I should swim in so I can find my father, but I won't leave the beach until I make sure you've returned to Connecticut."

I was sort of nervous about getting stuck here, but I said, "That's okay. You'd better get started."

"I'll wait on the beach," he repeated. "Well, bye for now. When will I see you again? Tomorrow?"

"Sure, I can't wait. See you then." I watched him head for shore. Tomorrow, I thought, tomorrow Davy and I—

It hit me. "Oh no! Tomorrow! Stephen, wait! Stop!"

He paused and looked back at me.

"The time thing is wrong!" I shouted to him. "When we left the island it was sunset, remember?"

"Yes?" he called back.

"Stephen! This is daytime! Look at the sun!" I pointed. "Stephen, it should be nighttime!"

He stared at the sun for a moment. "Then when *is* this?"

"I don't know!"

"Come on!" He began to swim toward shore.

"Wait, Stephen! Wait for me!" I swam after him as fast as I could. I might be zapped back to Connecticut any second and Stephen would be left here in some unknown time.

The salt water stung my eyes, but I didn't dare take them off Stephen. The blood pounded in my temples, giving me a headache. I was still panting and puffing like crazy when he reached shallow water and stood up.

A chubby man and a sunburned woman lay on lounge chairs back under the palms. Stephen shouted, "Sir? Pardon me, sir? Can you tell me what day it is?"

The man sat up and squinted at him. "You talking to me?"

"Yes, sir!" he shouted. "What day is this?"

"Whoo-eee!" the man bellowed. "That must have been some party you were at! It's Sunday, son, the day that comes after Saturday-night parties!" He laughed. "Did you hear that, Mildred?" He turned and poked his wife.

Totally panicked, I put on one last burst of speed, caught up to Stephen, and grabbed his arm.

An instant later we sprawled on the floor of my room, a white-faced Davy looking down at us.

Gasping, I managed to say, "Stephen, how would you like to spend the night in Connecticut?"

chapter seven

Davy threw himself on me. "I was scared! You got thin!"

"What?" I struggled to sit up with Davy clinging to my neck. "What do you mean, thin?"

"Like a ghost," he sobbed. "I thought you were dead!"

"I say, old man," Stephen said. "It's all right, you know. Here we are, quite alive, even if we are a bit discombobulated."

Davy stopped crying. "What does disabob-a-lated mean?"

"It means," I said, standing up, "that this magic business is making us *crazy*. Now, Davy, what happened when we were gone?"

"You were still here, but you *weren't*. I could see right through you. And you wouldn't talk to me or move or anything. You looked like a ghost! A frozen ghost!"

His lower lip began to quiver. I hugged him. "Hey, you were a ghost too."

"I was?"

"Sure, when we were swimming on Miracle Island, we must have left our ghosts here. What if Miss Cuddy found us like that?"

"She would've screamed!" He grinned.

"Did you scream?"

"No, but I was scared."

"See? You were very brave, Davy. Much braver than Miss Cuddy. You were scared, but you didn't scream. You remembered what to do. You called me back and here we are!"

"Yeah." He nodded. "I was brave, wasn't I?" He thought about this for a moment, then suddenly looked up at Stephen. "Hey, how come you came back?"

Stephen had put on Dad's robe and was standing at the window, watching the snow drift down. "There were complications."

"Stephen, if it's tomorrow on the island," I said, "that means you'll have to stay here tonight."

"Why do you say that?" he mumbled, gazing around my room.

"Look at it from your father's point of view," I said. "The last time he saw you, you were headed for the beach on Saturday afternoon. The next time you show up, it's Sunday morning. Won't he be upset if you just disappear overnight?"

"Quite upset. In fact, he'd be furious! And I couldn't blame him."

"But if you stay here," I pointed out, "you could call him and explain you won't be back until tomorrow."

"And say what? Hello, Father, I'm spending the night in Connecticut?"

"Are you sleeping over?" Davy asked.

"I'm afraid I have no choice." His grin flashed. "This magic business has a major flaw. When we went back just now, it was tomorrow on the island."

"How could it be tomorrow?" Davy said.

"That's what we'd like to know!"

I shivered. "Good thing I reached you in time."

"I owe you my eternal gratitude." He bowed like Shakespeare. Too bad he didn't have a plumed hat—it would have been perfect.

"You're welcome." I shivered again. A wet bathing suit doesn't quite make it in Connecticut, at least not in February. "I think I'd better take a shower, or would you rather go first, Stephen?"

"No, you go ahead. What I'd really like is something to eat, if you don't mind. I tend to become hungry whenever I travel long distances."

I smiled and pointed to my desk. "The soup is cold by now, but have some crackers. Davy, sneak down to the kitchen and find some more food for Stephen. And don't let Miss Cuddy catch you."

"Okay, I'm hungry too." Davy left and I collected some clean clothes. I also slipped my great-grandmother's letter into a pocket when Stephen wasn't looking.

"What are you going to tell your father?" I asked as I went toward the door.

"*I wish I knew.* I'm quite good with math and the sciences, but creating stories has always been a weakness. I gave up trying when I was eight and Father caught me with a stolen sack of biscuits. I claimed the birds had asked me to make crumbs for them, but since my cheeks were full and bits of biscuit littered my shirt, he chose not to believe me."

I laughed. "Don't worry, Carly and I will think of something. We make up terrific stories together. I'll call her and tell her to come over as soon as she finishes baby-sitting."

"Who is Carly?"

"My best friend. Don't worry, she's a world-champion fibber. You'll see when you meet her."

"Jenny, is it a good idea to tell anyone else about these, er, magical flights?"

"Carly's not just anyone. We have to tell her, first because she's my best friend, and second because we need her. You should hear some of the stories we make up together. Last year we won the Tall Tales contest at the library."

"Tall tales?"

"You know, like Paul Bunyon." I began to explain the idea and ended up telling him the whole story, Babe the blue ox and all.

When I finally got to the bathroom I locked the door and took out my great-grandmother's letter. The paper was yellowed and the faint, spidery handwriting hard to make out, with capital letters sprinkled around in odd places.

Squinting, I read:

My Dearest Child,

The Garnet Ring that accompanies this Letter has been in our Family for a great many Generations and is always . . . Did it say gassed? No, *passed on to a Blood descendant. There is only one condition as to Who may inherit: It must be worn on the Third Finger of the right Hand and it must fit perfectly. It must never be Altered, neither made larger nor smaller.*

The Ring was given to me by my Grandmother, as it was too . . . Snail? No . . . *small for my Mother's Hand. And I Give it to you, as it was too large for both my Daughter and my Granddaughter. We have met Only once . . .*

When? I wondered. I didn't remember meeting her at all. I must have been just a baby.

. . . under Trying circumstances, but I Trust that you shall grow to be more Worthy of the Powers.

Take Special Care with this Ring. . . .

That was where I'd stopped reading before. I still felt kind of annoyed about that "grow to be more worthy" comment. What did I do as a baby, spit up on her or something? But even so, I was dumb not to have finished reading the letter.

You will Discover its many Wonders yourself, as that is part of the Joy in its ownership. But . . . I couldn't make out the word. Was it *heed* or *read me well?* Oh well, same thing. *You must never confide its Secrets, even to Soul mates. Some might Guess, but you must never Utter the words. . . .* Good thing I didn't tell Stephen. *The Power will never Vanish, if you Abide by this Law.*

I add four Cautions. Take care when you choose the Medium, as you will arrive Precisely when and where the medium Dictates, in Increments of three, three, and eighteen. . . . What did she mean—medium and increments?

And while the Way is forged only by exigency . . . What the heck did that mean? . . . *take Care not to abuse the path for* . . . another word I couldn't make out—it was in the crease of the paper. I think it said, *Nancy's sake.* Or was it *Candy's sake*? Oh well, I didn't know any Nancys, and there was no way I'd ever trade it for candy.

And take Care when you choose your Returning friend, as she or he must be completely Trustworthy. . . . Returning friend? *And for you, Jennifer, I add a special Caution: take extra Care with your little brother.* I always take good care of Davy! Well, almost always.

With all my Heart I hope that you will Treasure this wondrous Ring, as I do. Use it Wisely and it will serve you Well. It was signed, *Ophelia Anne Cavanaugh.*

I reread the letter, then read it again until I'd practically memorized it. It told me a little, but not nearly enough. I had to "discover its many wonders" all by myself. What could the ring do, besides take me to Miracle? And what the heck was the "medium" and those "increments" and "exigency"? Why did she have to use such fancy words? I could guess what most of them meant, but what was wrong with plain old English? "Returning friend" was easier. It probably meant the person who called me back. I'd have to remember not to use anyone named Nancy.

Why didn't Ophelia Anne Cavanaugh write me an instruction book instead of this say-nothing letter? I mean, if you find a lamp with a genie in it, you know you have three wishes and that's it. Even fairy tales taught you more than this.

Maybe Great-Grandma Ophelia didn't want to say much because she didn't want the wrong people reading it, even though the wax seal on the envelope was unbroken until I opened it. Maybe she was just a cautious type of person. Or maybe you learned to be careful when you had the ring as long as she did.

I sighed, stuffed the letter back in my pocket, and went to call Carly before I took a shower. Maybe she could help me figure out what it all meant, without her knowing it, of course. Like Ophelia, I too would be mysterious and keep the secret of the ring.

Carly made it to our house from the Cranes' by 5:13, a new record. She burst in the kitchen door huffing and puffing, her frizzy red hair practically electric with excitement.

"What are the surprises?" she demanded, not bothering to say hello. "Are they about Bethany's party? Tell me! Tell me!"

"It's not the party. It's something else." I nodded toward Miss Cuddy, who stood at the stove, her back to us. "Come up to my room."

Miss Cuddy turned around and glared at me. "Jennifer, why didn't you ask me if you could have a friend over? You've had a relapse and are sick. You mustn't spread your germs around."

"I'm not sick!" I said without thinking. "I feel great!"

She clanked down a pot. "Good grief, look at your face! It's bright red!"

"It's the sun—" Whoops! "Th-the sunlamp. I—I was using Mom's sunlamp and I must have stayed under too long." Quick, change the subject. "Um, Miss Cuddy, you've met my friend Carly, haven't you?"

"I have." She looked grim. "I'm not likely to forget a person I met yesterday." She turned back to the stove and we tried to sneak out of the kitchen. "Are you sure you're not sick?"

"I'm positive. I thought my cold *might* be coming back, but it didn't." I'd blown the perfect excuse to keep the dragon away from my bedroom—and Stephen—but it was the only way Carly would be allowed to stay. "Uh, listen, we're going up to my room now. Call me when it's time to set the table, okay?"

Upstairs, I stopped outside my door, hand on the knob. "Are you ready, Carly? I told you I had a surprise—"

"You said *two* surprises. Two!"

"Yup, two of the biggest surprises you've ever had in your whole life. Ready for the first one?"

She nodded. I opened the door. Stephen stood up. Funny-faced, tan Stephen, almost naked under Dad's white robe.

The look on Carly's face was worth buckets of diamonds, acres of emeralds, pounds of pearls. In short, it was priceless.

"Hello," Stephen said. "You must be Carly. I'd offer to shake hands, but I'm afraid I'm rather sticky." He pointed to a jar of peanut butter, Davy's idea of a perfect snack. "Delicious stuff, but rather messy."

For the first time since I'd known her, Carly was speechless.

I gave her a poke. "Carly, this is Stephen. Stephen, my best friend, Carly."

"Hi," she choked out, looking at me. With one glance she asked, *Who is he? Where did you find him? What is he doing in your bedroom?*

"Sit down, Carly." I closed and locked the door. "Are you ready for the second surprise?"

"Awwk." She sounded like a penguin.

In the next fifteen minutes, Carly must have "awwked" thirty times. When I showed her the seaweed in the paper cup, she double-awwked. Finally I finished my story and sat down.

She looked from me to Stephen and back to me again. "Let me get this straight. This is not a joke, right?"

"Right," I said.

"This is for real?"

"For real."

"This really happened?"

"It really happened."

She stared at me, then at Stephen, then back at me. "You're sunburned," she accused.

"Yes."

Back to Stephen. "Is Jenny telling me the truth?"

"Yes."

She glared at me. "You've shown me a dried-up piece of seaweed, a sprinkle of sand on your carpet, a sunburn . . . and you expect me to *believe* this?"

"Yes."

Back to the stares. Finally she said, "Okay, prove it. Take me to Miracle Island."

"I will, Carly, I will. First thing tomorrow."

"Let's go now."

"We can't. Remember the time thing? If we went now it would be tomorrow—probably—and I don't want to mess around with tomorrow if we can help it."

Carly leaned forward. "But you promise you'll take me first thing in the morning?" She laughed. "Listen to me! I sound like I really believe in this magic of yours."

"Carly, have I ever lied to you?"

"Lots of times! But I never believed you before."

"And you do now?"

"Sort of. Awwk! I must be crazy!"

"You'll see for yourself tomorrow. But listen, Carly, we need your help. How can we keep Miss Cuddy from finding out about Stephen?"

She leaned back and thought a moment. "Maybe we should introduce him to her."

"As who?" I asked.

"My brother."

"But he doesn't look—or sound—anything like you."

"Then he can be my cousin, visiting from . . . let's see, what country is British and good for suntans?" She thought a moment. "India!"

"India isn't British anymore," Stephen said.

"Okay, how about Bermuda?"

"That might do," he said. "As a matter of fact, I've been to Bermuda several times."

"Good, then you'll be able to talk about it to Miss Cuddy."

"She probably won't ask," I said.

"Well, if she does, we're prepared," Carly said. "Now, do you have any clothes to wear?"

"I'm afraid not," he said. "I seldom go swimming in a suit and tie."

"You can borrow stuff from my father," I said. "His things will be a little big on you, but we'll say that's the style in Bermuda."

"Okay then, now we need a plan," Carly said. "First, you should get dressed." She blushed a little, glancing at his brown, bare—muscular!—legs below the bathrobe.

"The next thing," I added, "is to call your father and tell him you won't be back tonight." I explained the problem to Carly.

"You can phone from the drugstore on the corner, Stephen," she said. "We'll collect a lot of change for you—we can't have the call turning up on Jenny's parents' bill."

"You'd better go with him, Carly," I suggested. "I'll sneak you both out the front door while Davy keeps Miss Cuddy busy in the kitchen."

"Then what?" Stephen asked us.

Carly and I glanced at each other. Here came the fun part. I began, "I'll talk Miss Cuddy into inviting my best friend to dinner . . ."

". . . and I'll say I can't leave my visiting cousin home alone . . ." Carly continued.

". . . and I'll say we should invite him too . . ."

". . . and I'll tell Miss Cuddy I'd be so grateful if she could include a lonely stranger who is far from home . . ."

". . . and I'll get Davy to beg and plead because he's never met a real live Englishman before . . ."

". . . and Miss Cuddy will say yes before she knows what hit her," Carly finished.

"Are you sure?" Stephen asked.

We nodded. Carly and I'd had a lot of practice at this sort of thing.

"But what happens after dinner?" he asked.

"Oh, we'll stay for the evening, of course," Carly said. "Then we'll leave, and Stephen, you can come back and sneak in the kitchen door, which Jenny will leave unlocked."

He shook his head. "You make it sound so easy."

"It is," I said. "Don't worry, it's a cinch."

Stephen frowned. "But there's still the problem of my father. Frankly, I haven't a clue as to what I should say."

"Hmm," Carly said. "Let me think. How big is this island?"

"Rather large, as Caribbean islands go. Perhaps seventy kilometers long and thirty wide."

"What's the rest of it like, beyond the resort?" I asked.

"The central area is hills and rain forest, with the resorts scattered along the coast. There are several towns, most of them on the northern end. We're stopping at a resort in the southern part."

"That's it, then," Carly said. "You met some friends, kids who live on the island . . ."

". . . and they invited you to go to town with them—whichever town is farthest away . . ." I added.

". . . only their car broke down and they can't bring you back tonight, so they've invited you to stay over at one of their houses until tomorrow," Carly said, triumphant.

Stephen seemed a bit dazed. "You two are quite a team, aren't you?"

"Yup," Carly said. "Will your father believe your story?"

"I imagine so. What about your Miss Cuddy?"

I grinned. "She doesn't stand a chance."

chapter eight

I was right. Miss Cuddy bought the whole story. And believe it or not, Carly and Stephen were such good actors that after a while I caught myself thinking he really *was* her cousin from Bermuda.

Miss Cuddy had made a big casserole, so there was plenty of food to go around. She insisted that Stephen have seconds (on top of all the peanut butter and crackers he'd put away!) and asked him a zillion questions about "his homeland." I couldn't tell which answers were true and which ones he made up.

Davy—thank goodness—was quiet. He'd had a busy day and a couple of times I caught him nodding off. I tried to take him upstairs, but he insisted he was wide-awake and only babies went to bed so early.

"Are the sands in Bermuda really pink?" Miss

Cuddy asked Stephen as we finished dessert.

He smiled patiently. "Yes, a pale pink, but pink nonetheless."

"I'll have to tell my sister. I've wanted to go to Bermuda for years, but she's always said the place was too hoity-toity."

"Not at all," Stephen said. "It's a charming and friendly island, really quite casual. And the natives all speak English, of course."

"Yes, that's very important. We took a tour to France once and what a waste of good money that was! You couldn't understand a word anyone said."

I had to rescue Stephen. "Um, Miss Cuddy, why don't you let us do the dishes tonight?"

"Why, Jennifer, how kind. There *is* a *very* special program on television I was afraid I'd have to miss."

"It's no problem." At once Carly, Stephen, and I jumped up to clear the table, as if it were a job we just couldn't wait to start. "You go right ahead and we'll take care of the kitchen."

Miss Cuddy hurried into the family room and we all relaxed.

"Whew!" Stephen took some plates to the sink. "Thanks, Jenny, I was beginning to run dry on answers."

"You were super, Stephen." Carly carried the casserole to the stove. "I think Miss Cuddy has a crush on you."

"Please." He groaned. "She's a bit young for me, wouldn't you say?"

"Miss Cuddy's *old,*" Davy stated. "Jenny, can we go back to Miracle Island now?"

"Not tonight." I rinsed off a plate and put it in the dishwasher. "We'll go tomorrow morning."

"Can we go somewhere else, then?" he asked.

I turned around. Carly and Stephen stared at me. We were all hit by the same idea. Why hadn't we thought of it before? *"Somewhere else,"* I repeated. *"Wow."*

"Why not?" Stephen said.

"Yeah, why not?" Carly said. "Go ahead, show off your magical powers, Jenny. You say you can go to Miracle, so why not California?"

"Or Rome?" Stephen added. "Or Hawaii, or Alaska or China?"

"But—but, I'd need a travel folder. Maybe." I was breathless, remembering Ophelia's letter. Didn't she say, "you'll discover it's *many* wonders"? Of course! The ring could probably take me anywhere—Australia, New Zealand, Peru. . . .

"Can't you find another travel folder?" Carly asked. "Or how about pictures? Any kind of picture might do."

"I don't know . . . maybe in Mom's desk . . ." I turned off the water and ran to the door. "I'll be right back!"

Mom kept tons of junk in the bottom drawer of her desk. Old birthday cards, letters, report cards, Davy's scribbled drawings; she saved everything. I pulled out the drawer and rummaged through it. A postcard! Two postcards!

I ran back to the kitchen. "Where shall I go first? Disney World or Canada?"

"Disney World, of course," Carly said.

"Yeah, Disney World!" Davy shouted.

"Jenny," Stephen said. "Are you sure you want to try this? What if something goes wrong?"

"What could go wrong?" I was so excited my hands shook. "Now, I'll try it by myself and you can all call me back. Then you can take turns coming with me. Yes, yes, Davy, you first." I turned over the Magic Kingdom postcard. It had been sent by an old college friend of Mom's two years ago.

"I want to come with you now!" Davy said.

"Let me try it by myself first, Davy. It won't take long—I'll just stay a minute, then come right back!" I put the postcard on the table, sat down, and began to concentrate. Hiding my hands under the table, I played with my ring. "Okay, Disney World, here I come!"

Nothing happened.

I stared at the picture, wishing, wishing, *wishing* to be in the Magic Kingdom. Still nothing happened.

I felt sweat break out on my forehead. I've never concentrated so hard in my life. And nothing happened.

The clock ticked away. The refrigerator hummed. I stayed in the kitchen. The Magic Kingdom stayed in Florida.

About ninety-nine years later, I looked up at the others and whispered, "Darn."

"I knew it!" Carly said. "I knew you were putting

me on. And boy, you almost had me believing you too!"

"Carly," Stephen said, "the magic is real. It works for Miracle Island. I swear to you, this morning I was in the Caribbean, and this afternoon, Jenny's magic brought me to Connecticut. Twice."

"Sure," Carly said. "And Rudolph really flies too."

"Who's Rudolph?" Davy asked.

Carly blushed. "Umm, never mind, Davy."

"Rudolph the Red-Nosed Reindeer flies," Davy said.

"Yes, sure, I know he does," Carly muttered. "I was talking about, umm, another Rudolph. Hey, listen, Davy, tell the truth now: did Jenny *really* take you to Miracle Island?"

"Yup."

"Are you sure?"

"Sure I'm sure."

"You wouldn't lie to your old friend Carly, would you?"

"Nope."

Carly sighed. "I'm outnumbered. Guess I'll just have to wait until morning and see for myself."

Stephen picked up the postcard of Canada. "Do you want to try again, Jenny? Maybe Disney World has a rule about nonpaying visitors. Perhaps Canada wants you."

I shrugged. "I don't think so, but what the heck, why not?"

Canada didn't want me any more than the Magic Kingdom did. I gave up. "Maybe I have to use a travel folder. Or maybe it's only Miracle Island. It doesn't look like I can go anywhere else."

"I wonder why," Stephen said.

"Who knows?" I shrugged, thinking of Ophelia's letter. I couldn't remember any instructions on how to choose a place to visit. "This crazy magic does whatever it wants. Look at the time thing. Why do I leave here at one time and arrive there at another?"

Carly looked around. "Do you have a pad of paper? I don't believe this stuff—remember that—but maybe we can figure out the time mystery." Carly was a nut about games and puzzles.

I gave her a pad and a pencil. She made two columns at the top of the page: *Time CT* and *Time Miracle Is.*

"Okay, Jenny," she said. "Now, the first time you went, last night, what time was it here?"

"I don't remember exactly. After ten, though."

"What time on the island?"

Stephen answered. "Late morning, perhaps eleven."

Carly wrote *10 P.M.? Fri.* and *11 A.M.? Sat.!* in the columns. "And the second time?"

"It was after breakfast, so it must have been around eight-thirty or nine."

"Island time?" she asked Stephen.

"Afternoon, perhaps two o'clock or so. Maybe later, it's hard to say. I'd been snorkeling—"

"Snorkeling!" I said. "We *have* to go snorkeling tomorrow! How much does it cost to rent the equipment?"

When Stephen told me, I practically choked. "Just for a pair of flippers and a mask?" Good thing I'd saved up some baby-sitting money.

Stephen flashed me a smile. "It's not cheap to visit Mirabelle. Of course, *your* method of transportation does cut down on the expense."

Carly turned a page over and started a separate list: *Take $$$.*

"Add sunblock, Carly," I said. "If Davy and I get any redder, Miss Cuddy will flip out. And we'd better make sure it's waterproof."

She underlined *waterproof.* "Okay, let's get back to the time. Third trip: when did you leave, Jenny?"

"Davy and I left after lunch, so it was about quarter of one."

"And it was around five when you two suddenly popped up in the water," Stephen added.

"Gosh, you must have freaked when you saw us."

"Not really. By then I was getting used to it." He laughed. "Now, on the first occasion, when you went swimming in your pajamas, I admit, I did question my sanity."

My ears went hot. "Those stupid pajamas," I muttered.

"Actually, I thought you looked rather . . . intriguing."

"I looked ridiculous!"

"Not at all—"

"Hey, you guys," Carly said. "We'll never get this figured out if you don't pay attention."

"Yes, ma'am," he said. "Where are we?"

She looked at her notepad. "Okay, first you left here at ten-something Friday night and arrived on the island about eleven Saturday morning. Then you left again at eight-thirty or nine A.M. on *our* Saturday morning and arrived at two or later the same day. The third time it was quarter to one and five o'clock, and the last time it was—"

"Tomorrow!" Stephen and I said together.

"Wow, that's weird." Carly squinted at us. "You guys *have* to be putting me on."

"We're not, Carly, *honest.*" I touched her arm. "That's what happened, cross-my-heart-and-hope-to-die."

She sighed. "All right, all right. I believe you. I think." She wrote down *tomorrow.* "Wait a minute, what time tomorrow?"

"I don't know," I said.

"Perhaps we can figure it out, Jenny," Stephen said. "The sun was almost overhead. Remember? You said to remind you to bring sunglasses next time."

I pointed at Carly and she wrote *sunglasses* on the list. "So it was bright, but what time was it?"

"It had to be morning, late morning," Stephen said. "The man I spoke to plays golf after lunch. He's only on the beach in the morning and late afternoon."

Carly looked up at him. "So it was like eleven, eleven-thirty?" He nodded. "And you left here when, Jenny?"

"Around three, I think."

Carly put the last numbers in the columns. We sat and stared at them. They didn't make sense.

Time Conn.	*Time Miracle Is.*
10ish P.M. Fri.	11? A.M. Sat.!
8:30–9 A.M. Sat.	2? P.M. Sat.
12:45 afternoon Sat.	5ish P.M. Sat.
3ish " Sat.	11? A.M. Sun.!

"Just a moment," Stephen said. "Wait . . . yes, I see. . . ."

"What?" I asked.

"If you look at the difference in time between when you left Connecticut and the time you popped up on the island, there's no pattern. *But* if you look only at the second column, *Time: Miracle Is.,* there *is* a pattern. Eleven, two, five, and eleven again."

"That's right," Carly said. "It's every three hours, except you skip the night and go straight into tomorrow."

I caught my breath. The letter said "increments of three, three, and eighteen." So Ophelia meant *hours*! After the first time, we went back three hours later, then three more, then jumped ahead to eighteen. I started to explain it to Stephen and Carly, then remembered I had to keep the ring secret. And I couldn't tell them about the letter without mentioning the ring.

"But why every three hours?" Carly asked.

Stephen shook his head. "As you Americans would say, beats me."

"You know," Carly said. "I'm beginning to think you guys are telling the truth. How could anyone make up something this weird?"

Miss Cuddy pushed open the kitchen door. "Jennifer, I thought you said you would do the dishes. Look at this mess. And why isn't David in bed?"

Davy had quietly fallen asleep in his chair. "Um," I said. "I was just about to take him up." Why didn't the old dragon put him to bed herself? Boy, Mom and Dad were sure going to hear from me.

When I got back downstairs, Carly and Stephen were washing the pots. Carly saw me. "Hey, Jenny, we'd better go as soon as we finish up here. It's getting late."

When Stephen went to thank Miss Cuddy for dinner, Carly said, "Jenny, I didn't have a chance to tell you earlier, but Bethany called me this afternoon at the Cranes."

"Why?" I'd forgotten all about the Valentine party.

"She wanted me to talk you into coming. She knew you were really upset after the basketball game."

I put my hands on my hips. "Bethany doesn't care about me, she only cares about her dumb party. She wants to make sure I come so everyone will have fun giving me a hard time."

"Bethany's not like that, you know she isn't, Jenny. She told me to tell you she thinks Darren belongs in a sewer."

"She's right about that. But listen, Carly, I don't know if I'm going or not. I can't stand to think about it. I'd much rather think about Miracle Island. Just wait till you see—"

Carly shook her head. "Jen, the party is real. Miracle Island is—"

"Not real?" I asked, grinning. "Well, you'll find out tomorrow, Carly Finnegan, you'll find out!"

Stephen returned and the two of them left. He was going to walk Carly home, so he wouldn't be back for at least fifteen minutes. I made sure the kitchen door was unlocked, then went up and spread out a sleeping bag behind Davy's bed. If Miss Cuddy glanced in his room, she wouldn't see an extra person hidden back there.

The dragon was buried in a Cary Grant movie. I waited for Stephen in the dark kitchen. Waiting is not my favorite way to spend time. Finally I heard him at the door. His breath came out in frosty puffs and he was sprinkled with snow. I double-checked on Miss Cuddy, then we crept up the stairs to my room.

Safely inside with the door locked, he took off Dad's coat and rubbed his hands. "Coldest Caribbean vacation I've ever enjoyed."

I suddenly felt awkward, now that we were alone together. Up until now, Stephen had been a friend, sort of a pal, even if he was a boy. Now, I realized . . . he definitely was a boy! A funny-faced boy with elephant ears and a deep tan and great muscles and that incredible grin.

He was waiting. I had to say something. "H-have you been to the Caribbean a lot?"

He sat down on the window seat. "Ever since my father married Suzanne. She claims the English winters are too damp, so Dad packs his laptop computer and we fly off to one island or another."

More silence. What do you say to a boy you barely know? Think, Jen, think! "What does your father do?" Safe question.

"Oh, he's a businessman. Investments. Boring, but it pays for little pleasures like Mirabelle and summers in France."

"Yes, I guess so." I felt shyer than ever. He was not only a boy, but rich.

"I must admit, it's nice to spend holidays around members of the fairer sex, as the poet puts it. One tends to forget how charming the female species can be, when you're locked away in boarding school for most of the year."

"You go to an all-boys' school?" Not exactly a brilliant question. But safe.

He nodded. "Since I was eight years old. I often think that if I didn't have sisters, I wouldn't have a clue as to what girls are all about."

"How many sisters do you have?" Another safe question.

"Two. Elizabeth is married now, and Margaret will be attending university next year, unless she leaves school."

"Why would she leave?" I was curious.

"She wants to be onstage. She's really quite a good

actress, but she's terribly bright and also has a beautiful voice. My father wants her to get her degree while she studies for the opera. At the moment they're having rather a battle over it. But I don't want to bore you with family problems."

"I'm not bored." I wasn't.

He changed the subject anyway. "Tell me about your family."

I shrugged. "There's not much to tell. We're pretty normal. My father teaches English at the high school and my mother is a computer consultant. You already know Davy."

"He's a nice boy, and you're very good with him."

I was glad Stephen liked Davy. I was rather proud of him myself. "I've had a lot of practice taking care of him. I was seven when he was born, so I helped Mom from the beginning. He can be a pain at times, but I guess all little brothers are."

"So my older sisters tell me!" Stephen grinned and that tingly feeling washed all through me, leaving me feeling kind of weak and shivery.

He didn't seem to notice. "I say, I like your friend Carly too. She must be Irish with that carrot-colored hair and the gift of the gab. How do you two dream up such wonderful stories?"

"I—I don't know. We—we've always done it, ever since we met in s-second grade."

"What's the matter? You're looking odd. Come and sit next to me."

I sat down on the far end of the window seat. He

took my hand and pulled me closer. "What's the problem?" he asked.

I just looked at him. What could I say?

"You seem to be afraid of me. Are you?"

"Oh no!"

He kissed my cheek. "Good. Because I've been wanting to do that all day."

"You're kidding!" What a *dumb* thing to say.

"No, I'm not kidding. You know, I haven't kissed many girls, but there's something quite special about you. When I first saw you appear on the island, I was simply curious about your, er, mysterious appearances, but now that we've spent time together, I, well, I'm awfully glad we met."

"You are? Why?" *Dumb!*

"Because you're *you.* And you're a . . . a . . . special person."

"I-I'm just ordinary."

"Not ordinary. Extra-ordinary. Extraordinary." He squeezed my hand, then stood up. "And now you'd better show me where I'm to sleep, before your Miss Cuddy ends her affair with Cary Grant."

Miss Cuddy's name jolted me out of my daze. Or whatever state I was in. I became the efficient hostess, finding clean towels and a pillow, showing Stephen the hidden sleeping bag, standing guard outside the bathroom while he washed up. Mom would have been proud of me. Sort of.

Stephen slipped into Davy's dark room and whispered, "Good night." I stood in the hallway, my heart thudding as he closed the door. I didn't move. Couldn't move. The door opened. He kissed my nose. "Good night again."

The door closed.

chapter nine

The morning sun was too bright. I rolled over and buried my face in the pillow.

"Jenny!" Davy banged my door open. "Get up! Get up!"

"Uhhhnnngh."

The bed shook as Davy jumped on it. "Get up! We're going to Miracle Island!"

I sat up with a jerk. "Shhh! Don't let Miss Cuddy hear you."

"Okay," he whispered. "But Stephen's hungry and—"

"Stephen!" How could I forget him? I'd spent most of the night not sleeping, thanks to him.

"We have to get him something to eat," Davy said. "And did you see? It's stopped snowing."

"Yes, I see." I got out of bed. "Where's Stephen?"

"In my room, but he's *hungry*."

"Take him the peanut butter." I waved at my desk.

"Then run downstairs and see if you can sneak a banana or an orange out of the kitchen."

"I'll get both." He grabbed the jar and box of crackers and dashed out the door.

I took the world's quickest shower and got dressed. My heart was pounding like a heavy-metal band. Thoughts raced through my head so fast I couldn't keep up. Stephen had kissed me last night. *Twice.* Once on the cheek and once on the nose. Did that mean . . . ? No, probably not. He was just being . . . nice. But—did I remember right? Did he say I was special? No, he couldn't have. Yes, he did. And he also said I was extraordinary. He *did* say that. But what did it mean? Maybe he meant my magic. But maybe . . .

Stop it, Jen! Calm down. Take it easy. Be casual. Be cool. Deep breath, let it out. Now, open the door to Davy's room.

Stephen jumped up. "You startled me. I thought it might be Miss Cuddy."

"It's just me."

"Hello, me." He looked great in Dad's old college sweatshirt.

Darn, I was going shy again. "Um, Davy's trying to sneak some breakfast for you."

"Good. I'm afraid I've about finished off the peanut butter."

"That's okay. We have another jar." Great, Jen, what a brilliant conversation.

Stephen knelt down and began to roll up the sleeping bag. "Jenny, how old are you?"

"Thirteen."

He whistled.

"Why? What's the matter?" My voice squeaked.

"It's all right. It's only that I thought you were . . . older."

Panic grabbed me. "How old are you?"

He looked up from the floor. "Fifteen."

"Oh wow," I whispered.

"Apparently I take after my mother. We've always been mistaken for younger than we are. She tells me it will be an advantage later on, but frankly, right now I'd rather appear mature."

"But—you are mature!" I said. "I thought it was because you're British."

"How old did you think I was?"

"Maybe fourteen."

He laughed. "And I thought *you* were fourteen. *You're* quite mature too."

"I'm too tall, that's all." Why did I have to point it out to him?

"You're not too tall for me." He stood up, came over, and drew a line from the top of my head to his nose. "See? Just right."

"Just right." He was so close. His dark eyes were melty-soft. Oh wow—

The door banged open. "We don't have any more oranges, so I got you these." Davy held up an apple and a banana. "She's making muffins. I'll sneak you one after breakfast."

"Thank you, Davy," Stephen said. "You'd make a good guerrilla scout."

"People can't be gorillas," Davy said. "Gorillas are monkeys in *National Geographic*."

Stephen laughed. "Right you are. Sorry, my mistake."

"Miss Cuddy said to get you." Davy pulled my hand. "Our breakfast is almost ready."

"All *right*, I'm coming." I followed my pesty little brother downstairs.

Carly called about fifteen minutes later. "Listen, I'm going to pretend you're not kidding me about this magic business. I woke up this morning all excited about the trip. I still don't really believe it, but it's a lot more fun to think it's true. Just don't let me down."

"Don't worry, I won't."

"Okay, well, I have some good news. After church, my parents are going out to brunch with Dad's new customer, Mrs. Atchison and her husband. They'll be away for hours because they're going to this old inn way out the country and that lady talks nonstop and it'll take Dad forever to get in a word about insurance."

"So we can use your house?"

"Yeah, and we won't have to worry about Miss Cuddy. My brothers aren't home this weekend, so we'll have the place to ourselves. And I checked with the little girl who moved in next door, Tiffany. She promised to come over and call us back at noon." Carly was so excited that she barely paused to take a breath. "That will give us only a couple of hours on

Miracle, but Mom said I have to do my homework before Bethany's party at five, and I have an English essay due, so it should work out just right. Have you decided if you're going to the party?"

"No, I don't want to even think about it. Listen, Carly, are you sure using Tiffany is a good idea? How old is she?" Ophelia's letter warned me to be sure the "returning" person was "trustworthy."

"She's only eight, but she's plenty smart, and when I baby-sat her, she got into her mother's makeup—you should have seen the mess!—but I didn't tell on her, so she owes me one."

"I don't know, Carly. . . . "

"Jenny, relax, we can count on Tiffany."

"Well, if you're sure . . ."

"Sure I'm sure. Besides we have to have *someone* call us back, and no one wants to stay home. *If* we can go at all. How soon can you guys come over? Mom and Dad leave for church in half an hour. Can you be here right after that?"

"I think so. We'll have to wait for the right time to sneak Stephen out of the house."

"Stephen. Gosh, Jenny, he's so nice. Darren is just plain good-looking, but Stephen is much better than good-looking. And you know what? I think he really likes you."

"You do?"

"Yup. When he walked me home last night, all he talked about was you. Almost gave me an inferiority complex."

"He talked about me?"

"It was Jenny this, Jenny that until I was ready to hit him."

"You're kidding! But—Carly, I just found out . . . do you know how old he is?"

"I dunno. Maybe fourteen?"

"Fifteen."

"Wow!" Carly said. "He's *old.*"

"Too old for me, anyway." I sighed.

"Only two years. What's two years? When you're thirty, he'll be thirty-two. Big deal."

"Thirty? I'll never be thirty. And anyway, right now I'm thirteen and he's fifteen and those are *two very big* years. Dad would have a heart attack."

"Hey, listen, the guy lives in England. It's not like you'd be able to date him or anything. Unless he can afford an awful lot of plane tickets."

"But, Carly, your brother Pete is fifteen and he's always putting us down for being babies, calling us little twirps and tadpoles and stuff like that. So Stephen couldn't really like me. I'm just a baby to him."

"He doesn't act like you're a baby. A babe, maybe—"

"Carly!"

"Sorry." I could picture her cheerful, freckle-faced grin. "Listen, I didn't get the sunblock lotion because I have to stay home. I told Mom I wasn't feeling well so I could skip church."

"Okay," I said, glad to change the subject. "We'll stop at the drugstore on the way over. I'd better get going."

"See you."

* * *

Davy kept Miss Cuddy busy in the kitchen while I snuck Stephen out the front door. It was great to be outside. Fresh snow and blue skies, crisp air and bright sun. It was odd to think that the same sun was shining on both cold Connecticut and tropical Miracle.

Davy caught up with us in the drugstore and we hurried over to Carly's house. She opened the door wearing a wild Hawaiian print shirt over her bathing suit.

"I can't believe I'm so excited," she said. "Half of me knows this is impossible, but the other half can't wait to see the island."

"You'll be there in just a few minutes," I said. We followed her down the hall to her room.

"Now, tell me what to do," she said as she locked the door.

"You don't have to do much," I said. "We have to sit close so you're touching me, and look at the picture. Have we got everything? Towels, lotion, sunglasses, money for snorkeling?"

"Yup, and Tiffany will be here at noon to call us back. I bribed her with a trip to the Nature Center, just to be safe. She'll stand right outside the door and shout your name, Jenny."

"I want to stay on Miracle all day," Davy said.

"We can go back whenever we want," I told him.

Stephen frowned, started to say something, then changed his mind.

"Okay, let's do it." Carly plopped down on the floor.

"Show me the magic. If you can."

"Don't worry," I said, smiling. I couldn't wait to see her reaction.

We took off our winter clothes and huddled close together on the floor. I took out the travel folder. It was getting a little tattered by now.

Carly looked at the picture. "I wonder if the magic is in the folder. Do you think that might be the secret?"

"No." I shook my head. "It's only the thing in between, the what-do-you-call-it?"

"The catalyst?" Stephen said.

"The medium?" Carly suggested.

Medium! That's what Ophelia said in her letter! How did she put it? "You will arrive precisely when and where the medium dictates. . . . " I studied the center picture a moment, then suddenly realized why I'd left Clark Harbor on Friday night and popped up on Miracle the next morning.

Because the medium—the picture on the travel folder—showed the beach about eleven A.M. so that's the time I arrived: "when and where the medium dictates."

"Hey, Jenny, what's the matter with you?" Carly sounded impatient. "Are you getting scared that you can't pull off your magic stunt?"

"No, no, of course not. I just was thinking . . . um, ah, there's a lot of stuff we still don't understand about these trips." I shook my head. "But at least we know how to get to the island and home again. Everybody ready?"

They all touched me somewhere. Stephen's hand was on my arm. "Okay, look at the picture and pretend we're . . . where do you think we should aim for, Stephen? What's the safest place, where people aren't going to spot us arriving?"

"In the water, I think. Fairly far out. No one keeps track of the swimmers."

"Okay." I pointed to a spot halfway to the reef. "Now, think about being right here." We stared at the picture and I played with my ring.

We floated in warm water, blinking at the bright sun.

"Whoopee!" Davy shouted. "We're here!"

"Oh wow!" Carly was stunned. "It's true. It's really true! You weren't kidding!"

"Of course not." I tried to sound super-casual.

"Oh wow! Oh wow!" Carly shouted. *"Oh Wow!"*

"Hey, our stuff's bumping me." Davy pushed at the plastic beach bag bobbing beside us.

"Are we really here?" Carly said. "Pinch me, quick!" Davy did. "Ouch! Not so hard. Oh-boy-oh-boy-oh-boy-oh! This is *too much*!"

"Isn't it beautiful?" I said, like I'd invented the place. Well, in a way, I had. "Let's swim in to shore."

Stephen had been studying the sun. "Jenny, we must have used up the eleven o'clock slot when we came back yesterday. It's afternoon now, probably two o'clock. I'd better find my father. He'll be wondering."

"Okay, let's go." We swam down to the far end of the beach where there weren't any people and spread out our towels. We gave Stephen our snorkeling money and he left to find his father, promising to come back with fins and masks. While we waited, Carly and Davy dived in the water. I waded in and stood a few yards from shore, gazing at the palm trees, the flowers, the sea. This is the most beautiful place in the world, I thought. I wish I could stay here forever.

I forgot that people who own magic rings should be careful about what they wish for.

chapter ten

Stephen came back with masks, fins, and a small raft. He showed us how to defog our masks by spitting in them. Davy thought this was such a neat idea that he cleaned his over and over.

"Now, the first rule is: Don't touch anything," Stephen said. "Sea urchins and fire coral, for instance, have a terrible sting, but more important, we don't want to harm the reef. It's an extremely delicate environment. This reef is a national park, and you'll see a great variety of fish and coral because it's been protected. We have to do our part and not cause any harm."

"Are there sharks?" Davy asked.

"I've never seen one, but possibly you might see a nurse shark, or a sand shark. Don't worry about them. They're timid creatures, not at all like the great white in *Jaws.* These sharks won't bother you if you don't bother them. The same is true for the barracuda. However, it's not a good idea to wear jewelry when you swim around the reef."

I touched my ring. *"Why not?"*

"The glitter could make a barracuda think your ring is a small fish, and that means dinner to him."

Carly immediately began to remove her silver pierced earrings. I looked at my ring, afraid to take it off. And afraid to leave it on. I thought about staying on the beach, but I'd wanted to snorkel ever since I'd seen my first *National Geographic* magazine. Slowly, I slid the ring off my finger.

"Where should I put it?" I asked. "I can't—*can't*—lose it!"

"Put it in here with the rest of our things," Carly said, handing me the beach bag.

I glanced around. We were alone on this remote section of beach. *No one could possibly know my ring was in the bag.* "Are you sure it'll be okay?"

"Sure," Carly said. "Who could find one little ring in with all this junk?"

The bag was stuffed with towels, sandals, shirts, lotion, and sunglasses. I wrapped the ring in one of the towels and buried it at the bottom. My finger felt naked.

"Don't forget your watch," Stephen said.

"Oh. Right." My waterproof watch was plastic, but the sun did reflect on the glass. I took it off, zipped up the bag, and hid it under the hedge that bordered the beach. Stephen had said no one would steal it, but Mom always said it was better to be safe than sorry.

"Now, are we all ready?" Stephen asked.

Carly looked out at the reef. "Are you sure it's not dangerous out there?"

"It's perfectly all right, so long as you don't touch anything. And if you get tired, don't hesitate to rest on the raft."

We all nodded, but I guess we must have looked worried.

Stephen ruffled Davy's hair. "I promise you, it's quite safe and you are about to have the most marvelous experience you can imagine."

And wow, was he right.

We adjusted the masks and practiced breathing through the snorkel tubes in shallow water, then started out. Stephen swam sidestroke, towing Davy on the raft.

The fins made swimming fast and easy. I felt like a bird flying over a new country. Through the mask, I saw sandy deserts and patches of dark green grass swaying like miniature forests. Shells were scattered here and there, and twice I passed over schools of pale fish.

Then I saw reddish-brown boulders ahead. Close up, they seemed to be engraved with patterns like the model of the brain in Mr. Bomberg's class. I made a sound like Carly's "awwk." I was looking at brain coral!

And then coral was everywhere. All kinds of coral

and all kinds of fish. It was like I'd dropped into a Jacques Cousteau special.

Fish! Dark red fish; small green-and-blue fish. Silver fish with black stripes, splashed with gold on top. A huge red-speckled parrotfish hung under a ledge, biting bits of coral. Little red-and-gold fish darted in and out of caves. A long silver barracuda cruised below, totally ignoring me. I thought about my ring, back on the beach, then forgot it again as a huge school of flashing neon-blue fish swam slowly past the edge of the reef. They were so beautiful it was hard to believe they were real.

So many kinds of coral! Purple sea fans, rough pink walls, gray-green shelves, tubes like small chimneys. Coral that looked like flowers; coral that looked like moose horns.

I saw a daffodil-colored fish dash into cover below me. Taking a deep breath, I dove down to get a closer look and startled a small ray that I didn't notice until it swam off. I couldn't believe how gracefully it moved.

I rose to the surface and tipped my snorkel tube to drain it just as a cloud covered the sun. Suddenly the dark shapes below scared me. In a moment I went from feeling wonderfully free in a fantastic new world to feeling lost and panicky.

I looked around for the others. Carly was a few yards away. Stephen and Davy were a little farther off. They all floated, gazing down at the reef, with Davy hanging over the edge of the raft. I put the tube back in my mouth and looked down too.

It's amazing how fast "monsters" disappear when you see them clearly. The dark shapes turned back into coral, and in seconds my fear disappeared. The fish swam from here to there, going about their business as if we humans didn't exist. The sun came out and the reef exploded into light and color.

Carly kicked hard, chasing one of the yellow-splashed fish. It danced away, just out of reach. The moment she stopped, it swam along as usual, not at all bothered by the game.

I made my way over to Stephen. He was pointing out something to Davy. They were both so busy they didn't notice me. I grabbed Davy's flipper, gave it a yank, and he yelled.

"You dummy!" Davy sputtered. "You made me scare it away!"

"Scare what?" I asked.

Stephen said, "We thought we saw an octopus hiding in a cave. We were waiting for it to come out."

"And now it won't," Davy said. "Because of you."

"I'm sorry. Really. I didn't know."

"Well, we're not sure it *was* an octopus," Stephen said. "I say, I have an idea. Yesterday I saw a grouper further down the reef. Let's go see if he's still there."

"What's a grouper?" Davy asked.

"A *very* large fish." Stephen put the tube in his mouth. "Wait until you see him." His voice came out all bubbly and muffled.

We collected Carly and a few minutes later floated above the biggest, ugliest fish I'd ever seen. Stephen said it tasted delicious, but who could eat something that gross?

"What are those black spiny things scattered all over the reef?" Carly asked, hanging on to Davy's raft.

"Those are the sea urchins I mentioned. When they die they leave lovely fragile shells, but when they're alive, they sting like mad."

"I know, you told us," Davy said. "And you said barracudas don't bite and they don't."

The barracuda I'd seen didn't seem interested in (ringless) me, but I said, "They're awfully big, though, aren't they?"

"Everything looks bigger underwater," Stephen said. "But you're right, some of them are three or four feet long."

"That's big enough," Carly said.

"Look!" Davy pointed. "A turtle!"

We swam after it but couldn't get close, of course. This was his home, not ours. We worked our way down the reef, and after what seemed like ten minutes, Stephen said we'd been snorkeling for over an hour and it was time to head back.

We didn't want to leave, but we had to. As soon as I reached the beach, I ran to check our bag. It was still hidden under the bushes: my ring was safe. I put the bag between my towel and Carly's, then lay back and closed my eyes. I was tired from our long swim and the hot sun felt good.

"That was soooo *super*!" Carly said.

"Yeah, super-super," Davy added.

"Super-super-super-fantastic," I said, feeling lazy. "Thanks, Stephen, for taking us out there."

"My pleasure. But the reef should get the credit, not I."

"Did you see that big black fish with the yellow spot on his tail?" Davy said.

"And that huge red-and-green fish? Is that a parrotfish?" Carly asked.

"Probably," Stephen said. "They also come in green and pink, and light blue, and midnight blue. Rather obvious why they were named after parrots, isn't it?"

"Hey, Mildred," a voice said behind us. "These are the kids, I'm sure of it."

"Now, Harry . . ."

"I'm just gonna ask them, don't worry."

I opened my eyes and saw the chubby man standing over us. I sat up and nudged Stephen.

"I was right, Mildred," the man called. "It's them."

"Hello, sir," Stephen said.

"Where'd you go?" the man said. "Now, don't get me wrong, I ain't mad or nothing, just curious is all. One second you're asking me what day it is, and the next second you're gone. Poof! Gone! How'd you do that?"

Whoops! Were we in trouble! I looked at the others. Carly had turned into a statue. She'd been rubbing herself with suntan lotion and the bottle was upside down, squirting a string of goo on her leg. Davy started to speak, but before he could say more than "whomph" I'd clapped my hand over his mouth.

Stephen stood up. "Er . . . we swam underwater, sir."

"Naw, that ain't it. This here water's clear as glass. I would've seen you underwater."

I bit my lip. Stephen had turned pale under his tan.

The man lowered his voice. "Now, come on, tell me the truth. You ain't aliens, are you?"

"I beg your pardon?"

"You know, aliens, like from another planet?" He looked embarrassed. " 'Course, that's Mildred's idea. I told her she was nuts, but you know women. . . . "

Stephen shook his head, trying not to smile.

"I says to her, Mildred, that's only in the movies, but she says, so how did those kids disappear, then? Harry, she says, all those UFOs that people see, some of them have to be real. So, son, you tell me how you did it and I can prove she's crazy, you know?"

"Sir, do we look like aliens?"

He studied the four of us. "You look pretty regular to me, but then you never can tell. . . . "

Stephen was trying hard not to laugh. "Perhaps you would like to speak to my father, Sir Richard Harrison. I'm sure he'll—"

"Sir Richard?" the man said. "Sir Richard is your father?"

"Yes, sir. I'm sure he'd be happy—"

"Oh no! I wouldn't want to bother him, no, I wouldn't, not a-tall." He took a quick step back. "Now that I think of it, I've seen you with him lots of times." Another step back. "I'm sorry I . . . well, Mildred . . . you know what wives are like. . . ."

"It's perfectly all right," Stephen said. "I can quite easily see how you were confused. But when the sun hits the water just so"—he held his hand at an angle—"an underwater swimmer becomes invisible from shore."

"You're right! You're right! I didn't think of that! Sorry to have bothered you . . ." He took several more steps back.

"It's quite all right. Think nothing of it. Oh, and sir?"

"Yes?"

"I'd be most grateful if you didn't, er, mention the party last night to my father. You know how fathers can be."

The man pulled his shoulders back. "Of course, son. I'm a father myself and I know my boys have had a good ol' time or two they'd just as soon their daddy didn't hear about." He chuckled, then winked. "Mildred and me, we didn't see nothing a-tall, no, not *a-tall.*"

"Let's go, Harry," his wife called.

"Coming, Mildred. Nice to have met you-all." He trotted off.

Carly watched them start up the path. "That was fantastic, Stephen. Jenny and I couldn't have done better."

"Coming from you, that's quite a compliment." He wiped his face. "Whew, it was a bit sticky there for a moment."

"You were great, Stephen," I said. "Is your father really a 'sir'?"

"Well, yes. It's nothing to get excited about."

"That man acted like your father is important," Carly said. "Is he?"

"Some people are easily impressed by titles. My father is only a baronet; it's an hereditary title. One of our ancestors pleased the king hundreds of years ago and the title was his reward."

"What did he do?" Davy asked.

"Won a battle. Look, it's all very boring. Father is essentially a businessman who occasionally advises the . . . government." He turned away. "I'd rather not talk about it."

For the first time I suspected that Stephen was hiding something, but that was his business, right? I said quickly, "Can you believe that man thought we were *aliens from outer space*?"

"Did he mean like in the movies?" Davy asked. "Like *E.T.*?"

"That's right," Carly said. "Like in little green men from Mars." She put her hands on her head and wiggled her fingers. "See my antenna? I'm going to shoot you with giggle rays." She aimed at Davy. "Zzzzzzt! Zzzzzzt! Zzzzzzzt! Gotcha!"

Davy giggled.

"See? It works! I'm an alien from Mars!" Carly danced around, shooting rays and making green-men faces until we were all laughing.

Carly chased Davy into the water and I reached into the beach bag, looking for the towel I'd wrapped my ring in. I couldn't find it. Frantic, I began tossing junk out of the bag. No towel.

Davy raced past, dripping water and kicking sand. Carly stopped when she saw me. "What's the matter, Jenny?"

"The towel! The blue towel I hid my ring in! It's not here!"

"Is this it?" She scooped it out of the sand.

"Yes!" I screeched. *"But where's my ring?"*

chapter eleven

"Your ring?" Carly asked.

"Yes!" I shouted. "You saw me wrap it up in the towel!"

"No, I didn't. Honest! I remember you took it off, but I didn't see where you put it."

I groaned. "Why'd you have to use *this* towel? It was all the way down at the bottom of the bag!"

She shrugged. "So was the lotion. I don't know, I just grabbed it."

"We've got to find my ring! The ring is the—" I stopped myself just in time. "It—it's *very, very, very* important to me."

"Mommy gave it to her," Davy explained.

"I know," Carly said. "It's beautiful and it's probably worth a lot of money too."

"You have no idea what it's worth," I mumbled, picking up my watch. "And we've got to find it *soon*. Before Tiffany calls us back to Connecticut!"

Carly gasped. "Oh no, I forgot about that. How much time do we have?"

"Only twenty minutes." She didn't know that without the ring, we *couldn't* go back.

"I'm sorry, Jenny. I'm really, *really* sorry. Come on, I'll help you look for it."

"We'll all help," Stephen said quietly. "Don't worry, it must be somewhere nearby. Now think, Carly, you took the towel out of the bag, and what did you do then?"

She shrugged. "I used it to dry off. I wanted to put on more lotion because I was afraid it might have washed away while we were snorkeling, even if the stuff is supposed to be waterproof." Her eyes begged me to understand. "You know how easily I get sunburned."

"Where were you when you dried off?" Stephen asked.

"Right here." She pointed to a circle around her towel. Footprints dotted the sand, including the deep ones Carly and Davy had made as they raced around shooting giggle rays.

"All right. Let's organize a search." Stephen assigned each of us an area. "Run your hands through the sand; scoop it up like this and let it sift through your fingers. Dig deep, and make sure you cover every square inch."

Even Davy took the hunt seriously. We knelt down and slowly, slowly sifted through the sand.

"It's all my fault," I said, feeling sick. "I should have put the ring on as soon as we got back."

"Why didn't you?" Davy asked.

"I was going to, but I wanted to lie down for a couple of minutes. I thought the ring was safe in the bag. Then that man came over and I forgot about it until after he left."

"He was something, wasn't he?" Carly said. "There sure are a lot of crazy people in the world."

"Yeah, and I'm one of them," I muttered. "How could I be so stupid? Stupid, stupid, *stupid*!"

"Don't blame yourself, Jenny," Stephen said. "Any of us might have done the same."

"I don't know, if I don't watch out they'll give me the Nobel Prize for dumbness."

"But, Jenny," Davy said. "You brought us to Miracle. That's not dumb."

"Sure," I said, "but I can't take us home if we don't find—" *Why did I say that?*

"The ring?" Carly stopped digging. "You mean the magic is connected with—"

"No, no! I didn't say that!"

"But, Jenny, you can tell us, we're your friends—" Carly began.

"No, I can't! I can't tell *anyone.* If I do, the magic will—" I stopped.

Silence. We looked at each other. Then Stephen scooped up a handful of sand. "Never mind, don't tell us. It's not important."

"Right," Carly said. "I didn't hear *one word* about any ring." She looked around like she expected to see a fairy godmother hovering nearby. "Come on, Davy, keep digging. We want to find Jenny's birthday present, don't we? The ring is special because your mom gave it to her, right?"

"Yup." He nodded. I hoped he hadn't understood what he'd heard.

A cloud covered the sun. We sifted sand silently.

Our twenty minutes were almost up by the time we had worked our way all around the towel. I sat back on my heels and stared up at the sky. More clouds had rolled in.

"Now what?" I asked, scared.

Stephen sounded calm. "Carly, put the towel in the bag, then take it out exactly as you did before. Can you remember where you were standing?"

"Yes, the bag was here and I was here." She demonstrated. "The towel was rolled like this and I picked it up and opened it like this." We watched carefully. "I dried my face first, like this, then my hair. Then I walked over here. . . . "

"That's enough," Stephen said. "I should have thought of it before. The ring would have fallen out when you opened the towel. Let's search this area more thoroughly."

I glanced at my watch. "We're almost out of time!"

"We'll find it, don't worry. Carly, why don't you check the bag again, to be sure. Jenny, look under the beach towels too, in case the ring was pushed aside."

We scrabbled around on our hands and knees, bumping heads as we went over the same small area.

"I wish those darn clouds would go away," I said.

"It would be easier to spot the ring with the sun shining on it."

Stephen glanced up. "We may be in for an afternoon shower."

"Great," Carly said. "Just what we need."

Fat drops of rain began to fall the second she spoke. Were all the gods against us?

The rain fell faster. In seconds it was sheeting down, drenching us.

Stephen stood up. "Let's find shelter. We'll have to come back later."

"We can't!" I shouted. "Later will be too late!"

"I found it! I found it!" Carly jumped up, waving the ring. "It was in the bag all the time!"

"It couldn't have been! I looked!" How did I miss it?

"Here, Jenny, put it on! Quick!" Carly grabbed my hand and slid the ring on. "What time is it?"

"Twelve noon, exactly! We made it! Davy, Carly, hold on to me! Good-bye, Stephen, we'll see you tomorrow!"

Stephen frowned.

"What is it?" I shouted over the noise of the rain.

"Er, well, I haven't had a chance to tell you, but . . ."

"But what?"

"Well, I was going to tell you. . . . "

"Tell me *what?* Hurry up, we'll be zapped home any second!"

"I'm leaving Mirabelle Island!"

"What?" It was hard to hear him in the downpour.

"Our holiday is over! We've been here two weeks and my father, Suzanne, and I are flying home today! We leave for the airport later this afternoon!"

I sagged. It couldn't be true, but I knew it was.

"I meant to tell you earlier but . . ."

I glanced around. Everyone except the four of us had run for cover and the beach was deserted. It looked the way I felt: wet, empty, and cold.

"I'm sorry, Jenny." Stephen put his hand on mine.

"Don't touch me!"

He jumped like he'd been stung.

"I didn't mean it that way, Stephen. It's just that you might get zapped back to Connecticut by mistake. Again."

He smiled a little. "I liked Connecticut, actually."

Davy tugged at my leg. "Jenny, when are we going home? I'm *freezing.*" His lips were blue; he was shivering. Rain plastered his hair and dripped off his nose.

"Any minute now, Davy." I checked my watch. Tiffany was late, but maybe an eight-year-old wasn't totally reliable. Or maybe my so-called waterproof watch was wrong.

"You know what?" Carly said, shivering. "I'll bet it's warmer in the water than it is standing here in the rain."

"Good idea, Carly," Stephen said. "Let's go!"

I grabbed Davy and Carly's hands and we ran into the sea. It was like stepping into a warm bath. We waded out and crouched down in the shallow water. A few minutes later an amazing thing happened.

The rain stopped. Just stopped, like someone had turned off a giant hose.

"Boy, that's weird rain," Carly said. "Bam, it pours, bam, it stops."

"Ladies and gentleman," Stephen said, his arm sweeping the sky, "you have witnessed one of the wonders of the tropics."

"Is it always like this?" I asked.

"Pretty much, although some days it rains a little longer."

Davy tugged at my hand. "Jenny, when are we going home? I'm thirsty."

"I'm thirsty too," I told him. I looked at my watch, keeping a tight grip on Davy's hand. Tiffany was really late. In a way I was glad, because I'd never see Stephen again once we were zapped back to Clark Harbor.

But I was worried too. Did Tiffany call us too early, before we found the ring? Or did she forget her promise to Carly?

The sun broke through the clouds, flooding us with warm rays. At the same moment a picture leaped into my mind. I saw myself standing in the water, about where I stood now, shortly after we arrived this morning. I remembered thinking, I wish I could stay here forever.

I'd *wished* to come to the island. I'd *wished* to stay forever. Was I playing with my ring when I made that wish? *Did the ring give me my wish?*

I turned to the others and said slowly, "Maybe we're not going back to Connecticut. . . . "

"What do you mean?" Carly asked.

I didn't want to confess, but I had to. "I—I think I might have made a teeny, tiny mistake."

chapter twelve

"What mistake did you make?" Carly demanded.

I dug my toe into the sand. "Well, um . . . this morning, after we got here, I umm . . . well, might have made . . . sort of a wish."

"What kind of wish?" Stephen asked.

"Well, it's so beautiful here and . . . I—I wished that I could stay on Miracle forever."

"You're not alone," Stephen said. "I imagine many people feel the same."

"Yes, but I don't know if I was playing with—" I glanced at my ring.

"Oh," Stephen said.

"Oh no," Carly said.

"And the worst of it is," I said, more than a little scared, "I might have wished to stay here *forever.* That's an awfully long time."

We just looked at each other. The hot sun baked down on our shoulders. No one said a word as we waded out of the water and walked up to where we'd left our stuff. Shirts, sandals, towels, lotion, fins, masks, raft, sunglasses—everything was scattered about, soaking wet and coated with sand.

"I'm *still* thirsty," Davy said. "*And* hungry."

"Hey, Jenny," Carly said. "Even if magic won't take us home, we could ask your parents for help."

"Only if we get totally desperate," I said. "Can you see us trying to explain? Besides, if I said 'forever,' what if I can't even take a plane out of here?"

Carly frowned. "Maybe you didn't make that wish. Maybe Tiffany forgot. I sure *hope* so! I mean, this is a great place, but forever . . ."

"Darn this stupid old magic," I muttered.

"See here, Jenny," Stephen said. "We're forgetting the obvious. Can't you simply wish yourself back to Connecticut? It might cancel out the other wish, *if* you made it."

"I don't know . . . I don't think . . . but, heck, why not try?"

We sat down on the wet towels and Carly and Davy touched me. I played with the ring and concentrated. Nothing happened. I tried harder. Still nothing. Tried harder. And harder. Gave up. "Why can't this dumb magic follow the rules?"

"It appears to follow its own rules." Stephen said. "We simply don't understand them all yet."

"Maybe if we had a travel folder of Connecticut . . ." Carly said.

"Well, we don't." I sighed.

"I know!" Carly said. "If you *did* wish to stay forever, all you have to do is unwish it. Tell the ri—I mean the magic, that you *don't* want to stay."

I shrugged. What did we have to lose? Once again I concentrated. Closing my eyes, I thought, "I wish I didn't have to stay forever. I wish we could go home. Right now, if possible. Please."

I opened my eyes. We were still on Miracle.

We glanced at each other, then I looked out to sea. There was nothing to say. We'd run out of ideas. Davy began to build a sand castle. Stephen stood up and paced along the beach.

Suddenly Carly grabbed my wrist and looked at my watch. "What time did you say it was? I just remembered—Bethany's party starts at five o'clock."

"Party?" I said. "Here we are, turned into Robinson Crusoes, marooned on a tropical island, and—thanks to me—we may be stuck here forever—"

"Maybe not," she said with a cheerful shrug.

"How can you even think about the party?" I asked.

Carly grinned. "I like parties."

I just shook my head and stared out at the waves breaking over the reef.

Stephen returned from his walk along the beach and stood over us. "What shall I do?"

"What's the matter?" Carly asked, looking up.

"If you're stranded here, I *can't* simply go off and leave you! And I must, in half an hour."

"But, Stephen," I said, showing him my watch, "you will have plenty of time. It's only twenty after twelve."

"*Your* time! Connecticut time! Here on Mirabelle it's much later."

"Oh no," I whispered.

"Don't go, Stephen," Davy said.

"I don't see how I can. You might be here for hours, even days. What will you eat? Where will you sleep?"

People began to reappear farther down the beach. I began to worry about Mom and Dad showing up.

"Is there a place we can hide, Stephen?" I asked. "A safe place where we can wait while we decide what to do?"

He thought a moment. "There's an out-of-the-way spot, near the main building. We can sneak over there if we stay close to the cottages. We can probably make it without running into your parents."

"Let's go," Carly said.

"Yeah, let's go get something to drink," Davy said.

"Right. We're off, then," Stephen said.

We gathered up our sopping stuff and followed Stephen to a path through the bushes. Although I was sure it was too late, I hung on to both Carly and Davy, in case Tiffany finally got around to zapping us back.

Carly stopped to pluck one of the pink flowers that studded the bushes. Davy yelled at her. "You're not supposed to pick things!"

"Who said?" Carly stuck her tongue out at him.

"*Mom said.* I picked her some yellow flowers and she made me take them back to Mrs. Simon, and boy, was Mrs. Simon mad!"

Stephen ruffled Davy's hair. "You're right, Davy,

but you are allowed to pick these. They're hibiscus and each bloom lasts only one day."

The path led to a huge green lawn dotted with palms and umbrella-shaped trees. White cottages were scattered around, trimmed with vines and bushes bursting with flowers. Beyond them, a large red-roofed building spread out around a terrace and swimming pool.

"Whoa," Carly said. "This is some place."

"Yes, it's quite nice, isn't it?" Stephen said. "That's the main building." He pointed. "It has two restaurants, and there's a third built out over the water in the cove beyond."

"I'm thirsty," Davy said. "Can we get a soda?"

"Once you're safely hidden, I'll return our snorkeling gear and bring you something to drink. You wouldn't want to run into your parents, would you?"

"Yes, I would," Davy said.

I pointed. "Hey, look at that bird. See his funny yellow eyes?" We were in a big enough mess already. All I needed to make it perfect was for Davy to start looking for Mom and Dad. "What are those black birds called, Stephen?"

"Blackbirds." He laughed. "But officially, they're known as Carib grackles."

They squawked like rusty hinges and fluttered from tree to tree. Davy was so busy watching them he forgot about Mom and Dad.

I didn't. I kept swiveling my head, checking out each person in the distance, as we followed Stephen around the cottages. I felt totally desperate. What would happen to us if we were stuck on Miracle much longer? We'd be sure to run into my parents sometime. And what if—my heart did a deep dive—I had to stay here forever?

I thought of home and suddenly remembered that Davy had seen the ghosts we'd left behind when I tried to return Stephen to the island. Now there were ghosts in Carly's room. What if Carly's parents came home? What if they had a key to the lock on her door? What if—

It was too horrible to imagine.

Carly was so fascinated by the resort she seemed to have forgotten our problems. Stephen began to act like a tour guide and Davy and Carly hung on every word. What did they think? That I'd do all the worrying for them?

Stephen pointed out plants with exotic names: dracaena, frangipani, ylang-ylang, dieffenbachia, bougainvillea, ixora.

"What's that vine with the blue flowers dripping down?" Carly asked.

"Thrunbergia," Stephen said. "It originally came from India."

"Boy, you sure know a lot," Davy said. "How come?"

"I like botany and zoology. I plan to study both when I go to university, but that's a secret."

"Why a secret?" Carly asked.

"My father thinks I should take economics and join his investment firm. I want to work with endangered species in Africa or South America, but I haven't told him that yet."

"Why not?"

"I'm waiting for the right time. My father is accustomed to having his way."

For a moment I stopped scanning the grounds for my parents and looked at him. "But it's your life. You should be allowed to choose."

"He says there's too much political unrest in the world. He wants to keep me safely at home, in part because I'm the only heir to the title."

"You're going to be a 'sir'?" Carly asked.

He nodded. "In time. I have no choice. Here we are." He pushed aside a bush and led us into a small glen formed by the blank walls of several buildings. Even here there were lots of plants, including hibiscus.

I let go of Carly and Davy. It was after 12:30—definitely too late for Tiffany to call. At least, now that we were safely hidden, I could relax a bit.

"I'll be back shortly with drinks and food," Stephen said. "While I'm gone, Jenny, perhaps you and Carly can invent a story for my father, to explain why I'm not flying home tonight."

"You're staying?" she asked.

"Of course. Someone has to look after you. I don't suppose you brought much money."

"Only a few dollars." I felt suddenly glad. He wasn't leaving! "But, Stephen, what are you going to tell your father?"

"I'm not good at making up stories, remember? I

know you two will think of something. I'll be back as soon as I can." He disappeared through the bushes.

Davy began to build a fort with twigs and Carly and I spread our things to dry in the sun while we thought up a fib for Stephen's father.

Stephen didn't return for quite a while. While we waited I lay back on the grass and closed my eyes. In spite of my worries, I sort of sang inside. I was glad that Stephen was staying, and not just because we needed his help. Face it, Jen, I said to myself. You like him. You really, *really* like him. And it's not a crush, either. I'd had a few crushes before, but this felt different. It was the difference between biting into cotton candy or roast prime rib. Stephen was prime rib—solid, good, real, *there*.

But how did Stephen feel about me? Last night he'd actually kissed me. (Well, he kissed my cheek and my nose.) And then there was that moment this morning when he said I wasn't too tall. . . . But all day he'd treated me just like he treated Carly and Davy—friendly and nice, but not . . . special. Of course I *wasn't* special so why would he—

"Earth calling Jenny. Come in, Jenny." Carly tickled my foot. I yelped and sat up.

She looked around our little glen. "You know what's funny?" she said. "We really *are* Robinson Crusoes. We're stuck on a tropical island just like he was, only there are plenty of dry rooms and soft beds all around us, plus *three* restaurants full of food, and we're still no better off than old Crusoe. If it weren't for Stephen, we'd be in worse trouble."

"That's for sure," I said. "What do you think went wrong, Carly? Did we find the ring too late? Or did I make that wish to stay forever? I'll kill myself if I did!"

"Maybe Tiffany forgot." She sat down on the grass. "That's probably the reason, because every other time Davy or Miss Cuddy called you, bam—there you were, back in Clark Harbor, no matter what."

"Davy or Miss Cuddy," I repeated. "Oh no, Carly!"

"What?"

"I've never met Tiffany. Always before, it was someone I knew calling me." I remembered my great-grandmother's letter; she'd called the person "returning *friend*." "Carly, what if the magic only works if I know the person?"

"Awwwk!" Her blue eyes stared at me. "No way! That can't be it. Can it?"

I shook my head. "I don't know. But unless Tiffany forgot, or I made that wish, or we found the ring too late, that might be the problem."

She threw her arms out. "I'm tired of problems! Why can't we have some answers?"

"Right!" I jumped up and kicked the empty beach bag across the lawn. That felt good, so I picked up the plastic lotion bottle and threw it at the bag. That felt even better. I grabbed the pile of sandals and hurled them one by one, scoring a hit each time. Finally I felt a whole lot better.

Stephen's voice came through the bushes. "Give us a hand here, will you?"

I pushed the branches out of the way. He was

loaded down with a tray of sodas, a big bunch of bananas, and a large duffel bag over his shoulder.

We helped him with the stuff as he said, "I asked at the office if a cottage is available, but I'm afraid they're fully booked. And unfortunately, there's no other hotel nearby."

"Can't we stay in your cottage?" Carly suggested.

"The new people are checking in this evening. There is, however, a small island out beyond the cove on the other side of the resort. A chap named Joshua has a boat and he said he'd take us there, if we want. I'm afraid it's rather primitive: the buildings are in ruins, although one still has a roof in case it rains. But it *is* a safe place to camp out."

"Why don't we stay with Mommy and Daddy?" Davy asked.

"We can't." I didn't want to get into an argument. "Anyway, you'd rather go camping, wouldn't you?"

"Yeah, I love camping!" Davy said.

No tents, no sleeping bags, no marshmallows to roast . . . oh well . . .

---

chapter thirteen

Stephen passed out bananas. "All right, girls, what delightful story have you concocted for my father this time?"

"Can you leave a note for him at the main desk?" I asked.

"Yes."

Carly peeled her banana. "The note will say that your mysterious friends from last night—the ones whose car broke down—are going to give you a ride to the airport. Would your father believe that?"

He nodded.

"So he'll drive to the airport without you," I continued. "Then another message arrives at the airport, *just* before the plane leaves—when it's too late for him to change his plans—and this message will say that the old car broke down again and you'll be catching a later flight and would he please leave your ticket at the reservation counter."

"What a marvelous story!" he said.

"Do you think he'd get off the plane and wait for you?"

"I doubt it. I've flown a great deal and he knows that I'm quite capable of getting home on my own. He'll be a bit annoyed, of course, but he has an appointment with the Queen tomorrow. He couldn't risk missing it."

"The Queen!" Carly gasped.

"You mean . . . *the* Queen?" I squeaked.

"Er, yes," he said.

"Your father talks to *Queen Elizabeth*?" I said again. I couldn't have heard him right.

"She occasionally asks his investment advice." He was embarrassed. "Look, it's not such an unusual event."

Maybe not for you!" Carly looked at him with awe. "What's she like?"

"I've never met her, but my father tells me she's a most gracious lady. Please, I'd rather you didn't make a fuss. It's rather embarrassing. I should never have mentioned it."

"Uh, sure. Sorry." I looked down at my hands. My daydreams were hopeless. It was bad enough that Stephen was so much older, and so rich, and was going to inherit a title someday. Now I find out that he thinks it's normal to have a father who advises the Queen. My father advises his high-school students. *That's* normal.

"I love bananas," Davy said, helping himself to another.

"I'm afraid I've borrowed these from the blackbirds," Stephen confessed. "You see, they hang two or three stalks outside each restaurant for the birds, to discourage them from flying into the dining room."

"Do they come in the windows?" Davy asked.

"There are no windows, because there are no walls. The lobby, the dining rooms, the lounges—everything is open. You'll see when we go by on our way to the cove. We'd better leave soon. A security guard could stumble on us any moment. We won't be truly safe until we're on Cat Island."

We packed the extra bananas in our bag and crept out of the glen. There were a lot of people around, some in bathing suits coming back from the beach or the pool, some already showered and changed for dinner. A few were winter-pale; most were shades of pink and brown. I began to feel nervous, sure that we were going to run into Mom and Dad.

"I saw your parents on the terrace earlier, Jenny." Stephen must have noticed my frown. "They're probably still there."

I nodded, but my eyes kept darting around, checking out each face. Partway to the main building a drum began to beat, then another joined in. A man began to sing about a yellow bird and Carly moved in time to the bouncy tune.

"What's that?" Davy asked.

"The steel band. Quite good, aren't they?"

"Can we see them? Please?" he begged.

"Well, if you're very careful." He led us to a screen of bushes. "Stay right here and don't let anyone see you. I'll be back as soon as I leave the message for my father at the desk."

The band was grouped at the far end of the terrace, under a thatch roof. Tables were spread out around the clear blue pool, filled with people smiling, talking, and singing along with the music. I saw my parents with another couple down near the band. Dad wore a crazy-print shirt I'd never seen and Mom was in her white caftan. They both looked tan and happy.

Fortunately Davy was too short to see past the first few tables, so he didn't realize they were there. I began to relax, glad to know my parents were busy on the terrace while we made our way over to the boat and Cat Island.

Stephen came back in a couple of minutes. "Message delivered. Are you ready? Follow me." He led us to a sidewalk that circled around the building, then passed one of the dining rooms. It was open on three sides, just like he'd said. Waiters were setting tables, talking to each other in a musical language.

A long hallway led to the rest of the building. Just then my mother came around the far corner, headed straight for us. Her purse was open and she was trying to find something in it.

Talk about panic! I ducked behind a palm tree and

hissed to the others, "It's Mom! Get down! Hide!"

Carly took one look and threw herself behind a bush. Stephen grabbed Davy and pulled him behind another palm. But palm trees have narrow trunks. Mom would see us any second.

I peeked around the tree. Mom kept coming, still digging around in her purse. I ducked back, crossing the fingers on bother hands.

The suspense was too much. I had to look. No Mom. She'd disappeared. A door swung closed. I read the sign: LADIES' ROOM.

"Whooooo!" I let out the breath I didn't know I was holding. "Let's get out of here!"

Stephen swooped up Davy and we raced past the dining room, around a corner, and through a grove of trees.

"She didn't see us, did she?" Carly gasped as we ran across a lawn.

"Couldn't have," I panted. "Or we'd sure know it."

"That was close!"

"Too close!"

We reached the edge of the lawn and stopped to catch our breath. Davy's face was red with anger and he was almost in tears. He ran to me as soon as Stephen put him down.

"Jen-neee." He threw his arms around me. "Why did we run from Mommy? I want to *see* her."

I hugged him. "I know, Davy, but we can't right now."

"But—but—but I *want* to."

"I know you do, Davy, but how could we explain how we got here?"

"Maybe we took a plane?" He forgot his tears while he tried to solve this puzzle.

"Planes cost lots of money. How would we pay for it?"

"We could say we found a hundred-dollar bill on the sidewalk, like I found a quarter once."

"The plane costs more than a hundred dollars. Hey, look at that neat boat. Do you think that's the boat we're going to ride on?"

Stephen waved at a man on the small powerboat. "That's it, and there's Joshua." The man waved back and jumped into the water, wading to shore.

Davy looked up at me. "Are we really going for a ride?"

I smiled. "We sure are. We're going to have an adventure!"

"I love adventures!" Davy bounded down the steps to the beach.

I stood at the top of the stairs. A large cove spread out below us, with a sandy beach curving along it. Several brightly colored sailboats and Windsurfers dotted the water; others were pulled ashore for the night. The restaurant Stephen had mentioned looked like a steamboat with tables on the deck. A red-and-white bridge connected it to shore.

"There's Cat Island." Stephen pointed. It was far out in the bay and looked steep and rocky.

"Good," Carly said. "It's nice and remote. No chance of running into any parents out there. Look,

I'm still shaking." She held out her hand.

She was right, we should be safe on that tiny island. Almost running into Mom had given me a real scare. Out on Cat Island, maybe I could relax and take the time to think long and hard about the ring's magic. One thing was certain: I'd managed to get us into a terrible mess. Now—somehow—I had to get us out of it.

chapter fourteen

"You want to go to my island? Sure, I take you," Joshua was saying to Davy when we caught up to him on the beach. "You want to see my baby sheep?" He was slim and dark, with a gentle smile and he spoke in the musical island accent.

"Yeah, can we?" Davy's eyes lit up.

"Sure, no problem. Come with me." He picked up Davy and waded out. We followed, holding our bags high as the water got deeper.

Joshua lifted Davy into the boat, then jumped up between the two big outboard motors in the back. He moved like a panther, all smooth and sleek. I did a good imitation of a spastic giraffe as I scrambled on board.

"This is neat!" Davy said, exploring the cockpit.

"Nice boat," Carly said. Joshua smiled, shy and proud.

He started the engines, pulled up the anchor, and

whoosh! We were off to Cat Island with a roar.

We passed the steamboat restaurant and pulled out of the cove. The island grew bigger and I began to make out the ruins of several buildings on the hillside. Shouting over the noise of the motors, Joshua explained that they used to be guest cottages, but the owners decided not to rebuild after the last hurricane. Joshua used to live on the island with his family and take care of the place, but now they had to live in town.

"Why didn't the owners want to rebuild?" I shouted.

Joshua shrugged. "Who knows? Maybe too much money."

"I see the sheep!" Davy pointed at several animals quickly disappearing over the hill.

Joshua worked his way between big rocks just under the surface and anchored off a small pebbly beach. We waded ashore, balancing carefully on the slippery stones.

"How long you want to stay on my island?" he asked, starting up a steep path. He carried a heavy load of coconuts, but he climbed so fast we could barely keep up.

"I have to telephone the airport about five-thirty," Stephen said. "Could you wait and take me back then?"

"Sure, no problem." The path leveled out and he led us around a ruined concrete building. "Look, they want the coconuts."

A flock of chickens came running, squawking

and excited. Joshua disappeared and came back with a machete. "I feed them this morning, but they greedy." With one swing he sliced a coconut in half, then chopped it into small pieces that he tossed to the chickens. "Wait, the sheep come soon now, but you must be quiet. Not used to people, just me."

We waited, and finally a white sheep edged around the building, watching us with suspicion. Even Davy was quiet. She came nearer. Joshua tossed her a chunk of coconut and she gobbled it up. More sheep appeared, including the ram and a creamy brown mother with two tiny adorable babies.

"One week old today," Joshua said. "Pretty soon more babies." When they had eaten all the coconut, the animals wandered off and Joshua showed us the rest of his island. If we spent the night here, we were going to have to sleep on the ground because the buildings were empty. Most were falling down, but, as Stephen had promised, one still had a tin roof.

Joshua led us up the hill to the highest point. I forgot about the ruins because from here everything was beautiful. Trees and flowers grew everywhere. And all around us, water in a million shades of blue, so clear you could see right into the depths.

I began to wish that this was my island. I would tear down the ruins and build a new house right here. . . . I caught myself in time. Wishing was dangerous. Who knows, the ring might just give the island to me.

Stop it, Jen, I told myself. That's crazy. The ring isn't like that. All it does is take you to Miracle. It doesn't give away islands.

And how do you know? I asked myself. How much do you know about this magic anyway? Not much, I answered. Not nearly enough, and I'd better figure it out soon.

"What are you thinking, Jenny?" Stephen asked.

I glanced around. Carly and Davy had gone back down the hill with Joshua. I could see them way below, eating a yellow-and-orange fruit. Joshua cut another from a tree and offered it to them.

"I was thinking about this stupid magic, wondering why it didn't come with an instruction book," I said. Instead of an irritatingly vague letter, I added to myself.

"Ah, but then it would be too easy, wouldn't it? Isn't it more fun this way?"

I smiled. "It's fun, but it's scary too. Look at us; we're marooned in the Caribbean and I don't know how to get us home."

"Are you sorry you came?" he asked.

"Oh no! I'm *glad*. It's great, especially—"

"Especially what?"

I ducked my head. "Um . . . meeting you . . ."

"Why are you bashful, Jenny? You know I like you."

"You do?"

He laughed. "Of course I do."

"But—"

"Can't you tell? I like you very, very much."

I shrugged. "Well, sure . . . I like you too, but . . ."

He threw his arms in the air. "Don't you know what I'm telling you? I'm trying to say that . . . that, you're very . . . that I'm . . . oh blimey! I *like* you, Jenny! *Truly* like you."

"But you can't."

"Why not?" he shouted.

"Because! Because . . . you're so much older . . . and your father—"

"Forget my father! I can like you if I want to!"

"But why?"

"Why? I don't know why. You are the most impossible girl!" He shook me. Gently. "You're impossible and lovely and bright and fun and I like you very, very much."

"But—"

"Will you please stop saying 'but'! You like me, I know you do." He suddenly looked anxious. "Don't you?"

"Yes, but—"

"But what?"

"But you live in England and I live in Connecticut, and you're rich and I'm not, and you're going to inherit a title and I'm just an ordinary person, and—"

"You're not ordinary, I told you that last night!" He was getting awfully mad. "You're an extraordinary person!"

"But—"

"If you say 'but' one more time . . . I'll . . . I'll . . . oh blimey . . ." He kissed me. Softly. On the lips.

Oh . . . *wow!*

"What was all the shouting—whoops!" Carly looked up from the path below us.

Stephen and I jumped apart.

She grinned. "Sorry, didn't mean to interrupt you."

"It—it's okay." I felt my ears turn red.

"Oh sure." She shook her head. "Sorry. I was just coming to tell you that it's time to make your call to the airport, Stephen."

"Er, right." His ears were red too. "I'd better go along, then."

"Hey, I'm really sorry—" Carly said as we started down the hill.

"Okay, Carly, okay." I wished she would stop.

"It's just that I—"

"Carly! Okay!" I shouted.

She stopped. We went the rest of the way in silence.

Davy and Joshua were waiting on the little beach. "Jenny," Davy called as soon as he saw me. "Can I go on the boat with Stephen? Joshua says I can. Can I, *please*?"

"No, Davy, you have to stay here with Carly and me."

"But—"

"Don't argue, Davy." Little brothers—and best friends—can be such a pain sometimes.

"Here, Jenny." Stephen handed me a slip of paper. "In case you're gone before I return, this is my address and telephone number. Perhaps we could write each other."

"Uh, sure," I said. "But I have a feeling we'll be here when you get back."

"Then I'll see you soon." He hopped into the boat, Joshua cast off, and as they pulled away, Stephen winked and flashed me a grin. It warmed me like a hundred bonfires.

As the boat headed for shore I heard the steel band begin a reggae song, the music faint, but carrying over the water. The group must have moved from the terrace to the steamboat restaurant. We went back up the hill to watch the sunset.

"Anyone want a banana?" Carly asked, dancing in time to the music as she opened the beach bag.

"Sure." I took two and handed one to Davy. "I saw Joshua cut some fruit for you. What was it?"

"Papaya," she said. "It's delicious. But I guess you and Stephen had something more delicious."

"Carly! That's not funny!"

"Sorry. But didn't I tell you? Wasn't I right? He *does* like you."

"Umm." I busied myself with the banana. Part of me was chirping with happiness and the other part couldn't quite believe what Stephen had said.

The sun was just touching the edge of the ocean. Would we still be here to see the sunset tomorrow? Probably, unless I did something about this crazy magic . . .

"Jenny," Davy asked. "When are we going home?"

"I'm not sure, Davy," I said. "You know, it's not

really as late as it seems. Even though it's getting dark here, it's only two o'clock in the afternoon back in Connecticut." I rubbed his back. "Hey, smile, we're having an adventure, aren't we, Davy?"

"I guess so . . . but when are you going to take us home?"

I sighed and shook my head.

"Hey, cheer up, Jenny," Carly said. "At least you know how to bring us to this fabulous place. So what if we're stuck here a little longer than we planned? I've decided I like being marooned in paradise."

"But, Carly," I said with a shiver of fear, "did you forget? We left our ghosts behind, and your parents could walk into your room and see those ghosts any minute!"

Carly winced, then tried to sound casual. "Mom and Dad probably aren't home yet."

I just looked at her. She shrugged.

"And", I went on, thinking of the "many wonders" mentioned in the letter, "we don't know if the ri—I mean the magic, can grant me other wishes. Like wanting to stay here forever."

"But if you made that wish, you also canceled it when you wished *not* to stay forever." She could be awfully annoying when she was determined to look on the bright side.

"And worst of all," I went on, ignoring her, "we don't know what went wrong. Why hasn't Tiffany called us home?"

Finally Carly looked worried. "You don't think that

maybe . . . the magic . . . ran out . . . like a dead battery?"

"No." I felt relieved. The letter said "the power will never vanish" if I followed the "Law," and I had; I hadn't told anyone about it. I didn't "utter the words" as Ophelia put it. Carly and Stephen might have guessed (well, they *did* guess), but I'd never actually told them that the ring was the source of the magic. "I'm sure we don't have to worry about dead batteries."

"Good," Carly said. "Then we'll get home sometime, even if it does take a while."

I shook my head. Carly was determined not to worry. She was happy to leave that up to me. "I've got to figure it out, Carly. It's my fault we're in this mess. You're pretty sure Tiffany can be trusted, that she'd show up at noon?"

She nodded.

"Would she keep on calling us if we didn't answer right away?"

"She promised she would."

"Then I think the problem is that I haven't met her." I remembered again Ophelia's "returning *friend*." It seemed that every word in my great-grandmother's mysterious letter was important.

"That's good," Carly said. "Because, sooner or later, someone you know is bound to call you."

"Yeah," I said, feeling grim. "But who? And when?"

It turned dark quickly, just a few minutes after the sun went down. The resort across the water was lit up like a fairy-tale city, but our only light was a quarter moon, and the island was a little spooky. We knew the shapes that rustled in the bushes were chickens and sheep, but still . . .

"Hey, look!" Davy dropped his banana peel and pointed.

A small tour boat had pulled away from the steamboat restaurant and was headed out past our island. The open cockpit was lit by soft pink lights and covered by a striped awning. It was filled with about a dozen people grouped together in pairs.

As the boat drew closer the breeze blew an islander's voice across the water. "Welcome to our moonlight cruise . . . your chance for romance under the stars . . . please enjoy your champagne dinner and a little night music. . . ."

We saw him pick up a guitar and begin to sing one of those oldtime songs that Mom sometimes played on the stereo, about being in the mood for love. A man in a crazy-print shirt put his arm around a lady in a white caftan. My parents!

I turned to distract Davy, but it was too late.

"Hey!" Davy said. "I see Mom and Dad!" He began to run down the steep path to the rocky little beach.

I was after him in two seconds, but he was already yelling, "Mommy! Daddy!"

Stumbling down the slope in the dark, I caught up with him and clamped my hand over his mouth. "Davy, don't," I hissed. "Be quiet!"

He wriggled like an eel and I clutched him with all my strength. Some of the people on the boat had turned to look in our direction, but the boat was moving past the other side of the island and would soon be out of sight. I was pretty sure we were hidden by the darkness, but still, my heart was pounding like crazy from the scare.

Carly caught up with us just as the boat disappeared. Even though Davy had stopped struggling so hard by then, I kept my hand firmly over his mouth.

"Do you think they heard him?" Carly whispered.

"I guess so, but I don't think they saw us." My heart was beginning to slow down a bit. "Davy, hold still!"

"Mmmgghhtt." He tried to bite my fingers.

"Davy, cut it out. That wasn't Mom and Dad. They just looked a little bit like them." I didn't like to lie to him, but I had to calm him down.

"Wwwsssoooo."

"No, it wasn't," I said firmly. "Anyway, the boat's gone. Now, are you going to behave yourself?"

He stood quietly a moment and I knew he was thinking it over. Finally he nodded.

"Do you promise?" I relaxed my grip slightly.

He nodded again.

I let go.

A second later the bow of the boat reappeared from behind the island. All the passengers were standing up, looking toward our shore.

Davy was off like a speeding bullet, yelling at the top of his lungs. "Mommmeeee!" He tore down the slope and threw himself into the water, headed for the boat.

Carly and I raced after him.

Bang! Bang! Bang! My heart was thudding so loud it pounded in my ears.

We hit the shallow water together. I slipped on one of the rocks and my knee exploded in pain. Carly plunged ahead.

I tried to ignore my knee and the fierce pounding in my head as I splashed through the shallows.

Davy was a good swimmer, but he was only six. I saw Carly closing the distance between them.

Ba-boom! Ba-boom! My head was throbbing with pain.

I reached deeper water and began to swim, arms churning, legs thrashing.

The tour boat came closer, headed right for us.

Carly caught Davy. He began to yell, "Momm—"

She covered his mouth.

Ba-boom! My head weighed a hundred tons. I kept swimming.

Davy pulled free from Carly. "Mommeeee!"

I closed the gap. My hand clamped over Davy's mouth. Carly wrapped her arms around both of us.

Bang, bang, bang. The pain in my head was unreal. I moaned.

The pain eased up. I opened my eyes. Saw Carly's room. Carly. Davy. Sopping wet.

Carly's mother pounded on the door. "Carly!

Jenny! Answer me! Do you hear me? Carly! Jenny! Answer me!"

"Just a minute, Mom." Carly scrambled to her feet, started for the door, then turned to me. "We're back."

I nodded. "We're back."

chapter fifteen

I rang Bethany's doorbell, wondering why I wasn't nervous. Maybe because getting through a Valentine's Day party seemed simple compared with being marooned in the Caribbean.

Bethany opened the door and loud music poured out. "Jenny! Super! Come on in. Hey, you look great. Are you wearing makeup?"

I nodded. I'd borrowed some of Mom's stuff to try to cover my sunburn. "Sounds like a good party. Is Carly here yet?"

"Yeah, she came early because she has to leave early. Her mom's mad at her for some reason." Bethany led me down the hall to the family room.

I knew why Carly's mother was mad. She'd been outside the bedroom door, calling us over and over before we were zapped back to Clark Harbor. *Then,* when we finally answered her, she found us soaking wet, wearing bathing suits in the middle of February. Even though we told her we were just playing a game, who could blame Mrs. Finnegan for thinking something was weird?

At least we'd found out why we were marooned on Miracle, and, at last, I knew how to control the coming-home part. I was right. Tiffany had kept her end of the bargain, but it didn't work because I'd never met her. It sure worked when Carly's mom called me. I still had a little headache. I must have felt her yelling my name, but I didn't want to come back until both Carly and Davy touched me.

"What do you think?" Bethany stopped at the door to the family room and pointed to her eyes. She was wearing mascara to darken the pale eyelashes that went with her long blond hair.

"Looks good. You should use it all the time."

"Hah! My mother would kill me. How come you get to wear so much makeup?"

"My mom's on vacation." I grinned. Here I was, just back from my own little vacation on a tropical island.

"Hey, Jenny." Allison came over. She'd French-braided her smoky dark hair and was wearing a Save the Whales shirt. Allison is into the environment and I wished I could tell her about our snorkeling trip. "Are you okay?" she asked. "I was worried about you after that jerk gave you those polluted flowers."

"I'm great. Speaking of jerks, is he here?"

"Too bad, but yes," Bethany said. "I'd already invited him and Mom wouldn't let me uninvite him, even when I told her about that totally dumb trick."

I looked around the room. Valentine hearts and red crepe paper hung everywhere. Darren-the-jerk was sitting with two friends under a fat Cupid. He was laughing and joking, trying to pretend he didn't notice that everyone else was ignoring him.

"Want a soda?" Bethany asked. "Come on."

We had to pass Darren to get to the ice-filled cooler. As I walked by he made gross sneezing noises and his buddies laughed. I just kept going, pretending he didn't exist. He really was pathetic. Let him laugh at me if he wanted to. Who cared what Darren thought?

Carly stood by the cooler, talking to Scott Daniels, *the* cutest guy in the whole school, the one I'd never had the nerve to speak to. The sun had multiplied Carly's freckles by the millions and she looked great in her kelly-green sweater. "Hi, Jenny. How was your weekend?" she asked, faking an I'm-so-innocent smile.

I decided to play her game. "My weekend was . . . interesting. Very, very interesting, as a matter of fact."

The music stopped. "Ooops, the tape ran out," Carly said. "Bethany appointed me official deejay—back in a sec." She headed for the stereo, looking suspiciously smug.

I'd just taken a sip of cherry soda when calypso music poured out of the speakers. "Yellow Bird!" The same song we'd heard on the island. I looked over at Carly. She was trying to smother her giggles.

I wasn't so lucky. I laughed and soda spurted out

of my mouth. Right down the front of Scott Daniels's white shirt.

Scott Daniels. *The* cutest guy in the whole school. And I'd just baptized him with bright red soda.

"Oh wow, I'm sorry!" I grabbed a bunch of napkins and scrubbed at his shirt. "I'm so sorry, really I am!"

He stood there, watching me and grinning.

Suddenly I realized what I was doing. Here I was, rubbing the chest of a boy I'd never even dared talk to. My face flashed hot, then suddenly I burst out laughing.

"What's so funny?" he asked, still grinning.

"Nothing! No! Everything!"

"That's what I like, a girl who can make up her mind," Scott said. "Where have you been all my life?"

"Oh, I've been hanging around, just waiting for a chance to spit cherry soda on you." Could this really be *me,* Jenny, joking around with *Scott Daniels*?

Later, I danced with Mike Chang and Alan Roback, and let Jason Parker beat me at Ping Pong. (Well, I didn't actually let him—he has a wicked serve.) I must have been crazy to worry so much about this party.

Then Scott Daniels, cherry-stained shirt and all, asked me to dance. He's a great dancer—the best—and I was so busy trying to keep up with him I didn't notice we'd moved over near Darren-the-jerk. Suddenly I tripped and almost fell. Scott caught me, then pushed me to the side.

"You idiot!" he shouted at Darren. "I saw that! You tripped her on purpose!"

"Who me?" Darren said with a mean smile. "Better watch your mouth, Rotty-Scotty."

"Why, you dweeb!" Scott raised his fist. "I'll—"

I caught his arm. "Don't, Scott. Forget it."

The music stopped. Darren snickered. Everyone in the room heard him. Whirling around, I faced him. "Why don't you grow up? No one thinks you're funny except you! Your jokes were old in the third grade!"

He shook his finger at me. "Temper, temper. Hey, guys, look how mad she is. You're beautiful when you're mad, you know that?"

My voice turned icy. "What a corny line. Now I know how you waste your life—watching old movies. Old movies, old jokes. *Get with it, Darren.*"

I turned and walked away.

"Way to go, Jenny," Carly said, slapping me on the back.

"O*kay,* Jen-Jen," Allison said.

Scott came over. "Someday I'm going to smash that guy."

Bethany touched his arm. "Jenny's right, Scott, it wouldn't do any good. And hey, thanks for not starting a fight. My parents would've freaked."

Scott began to relax. "Yeah, it'd be too bad to mess up your party with that slob."

I smiled at him. "Thanks for your help, though."

"Anytime." He gave me a mock salute and a big grin.

The pizza arrived a few minutes later. Carly and I found seats in a corner of the room. "I have to eat fast," she said. "I've got to be home by seven or I'm in deep trouble." She shook her head. "Boy, after this wild weekend, school's going to be bor-ing."

Miracle Island and the magic flooded back into my mind. "It was super, wasn't it? But it bothers me that I didn't get a chance to say good-bye to Stephen."

"He'll understand. You can write him a letter."

"I wish I could visit him in England instead. Too bad the magic doesn't work that way." I sighed and took a bite of pizza.

Carly frowned. "You know, I've been wondering about that. Why did the magic take you to Miracle?"

"I don't know. I just desperately wanted to go. Mom and Dad were there and I wanted to be with them, and I definitely did *not* want to be home."

"Did you want to go to Disney World, or Canada, when we tried it last night?" she asked.

"Well, sure, but not as much. I mean, everyone wants to go to Disney World, but I didn't feel that awful need to—"

"Need to what?" she asked.

I held up my hand. "Let me think a minute." I reran the words I'd just said in my mind. First, I knew someone on Miracle, my parents. I didn't know anyone in Disney World. But maybe just as important, I remembered that aching, twisted-stomach feeling I'd had Friday night, that huge longing to escape Connecticut and be on Mirabelle.

Before Bethany's party, I'd reread Great-Grandma Ophelia's letter. More of it made sense now, but at least one sentence was still confusing. It read, "And while the Way is only forged by exigency, take care not to abuse the path for Nancy's [or Candy's] sake."

"I need a dictionary," I told Carly. "Do you see one?"

"There must be one here somewhere," Carly said, glancing at the bookcases lining one wall of Bethany's family room. "But why do you want—"

"Just help me find one. Quick!" I wished I could tell Carly about the letter, but knew I couldn't. We scanned the shelves and a minute later she handed me an old, thick book.

I flipped it open to the *E*s. "Exigency" meant an urgent want or need. On to the *F*s. "Forge" had a lot of meanings but one of them was to move ahead. I wasn't as lucky with "Way." It had so many meanings I gave up.

But now, at last, at least part of that sentence was coming clear. Did "the Way" mean how to go somewhere? Could I only "forge" ahead to a place if I had an urgent need?

"Carly," I said slowly. "What if I need a really strong reason to be wherever I want to go?" I described how I'd felt Friday night.

She twisted a strand of her frizzy red hair around her finger, thinking. "Makes sense," she decided. "Except that was only true the first time you went to Miracle. You didn't feel it so strongly the other times, did you?"

I slumped back in the chair. "No, not really. I wanted to go again, but I didn't have that horribly desperate feeling."

"Maybe once you've been to a place, it's easier to

go back," she said. "But I have another idea. Your parents were on Miracle Island. If you have to know the person who's calling you back, maybe you have to know someone where you're going."

I couldn't remember anything about that in Ophelia's letter, unless . . . could knowing someone be part of the "exigency"? Maybe.

Carly took a bite of pizza. "Actually, it could be either reason, or maybe both."

"Both!" I said. "That's too hard. I'll never be able to go anywhere else."

"Are you sure?" She grinned. "When Stephen gets back to London, you'll know someone there. And I'll bet you'll desperately, deep-down-inside want to visit him, won't you?"

I stared at her. "Well . . . yes!"

I felt stunned by the idea. Maybe I could see Stephen again. Maybe I could actually visit at least one other part of the world. Maybe I could make more friends—pen pals?—foreign-exchange students?—and see lots more places. Oh, if only the maybes were true!

"Carly!" My voice came out in a whisper. "Oh wow, Carly, Stephen should be home by tomorrow afternoon. I think." My voice went up an entire octave. "Tomorrow we could experiment and find out if I can go to London!"

"Shh, not so loud." She glanced around. No one was paying attention to us. "Stephen may not be back by then. We don't know what plane he's taking and you can't go to London without him. *If* my idea is right."

She popped a piece of pepperoni in her mouth.

I banged my fist on my knee, nearly dumping my pizza on the floor. "Why do we have to guess all the rules? Why can't the magic be simple? Like, three wishes and that's it?"

Carly's mouth dropped open. "You're *complaining*? Do you know a single person who wouldn't trade places with you in a second?"

"No, you're right. Look, if I pick up a travel folder right after school tomorrow, can we try as soon as you get out of swim practice?"

She finished her pizza and stood up. "Tuesday would be better."

"Carly! I *have to know* if I can go somewhere else soon! I can't wait until Tuesday!"

"Sure you can. Isn't your mom always saying it's better to be safe than sorry?" She looked at her watch. "Hey, I've got to go. See you in school."

Davy was in the family room, talking on the phone to Mom when I got home. I ran to the extension in the kitchen.

"I miss you too, Davy," she was saying as I picked up.

"Hi, Mom!" I gripped the receiver, wondering what Davy had told her. "I thought you said you weren't going to call."

"We didn't plan to, but an odd thing happened to-night. Your father and I were out on a moonlight cruise with several other couples. We were near a small island and we thought we heard a child calling for his mommy."

I crossed my fingers, praying Davy would keep his mouth shut. I'd already threatened him with deep dark horror if he said one word about Miracle Island.

"That was—" Davy began.

I cut him off. "Davy, remember what I told you!"

He fell silent. To Mom I said, "That's a strange thing to happen."

She laughed a little. "It turned out the other couples were parents too, and we each thought it was our own child calling us. It was too dark to see anything except a few splashes in the water. The guide said that was fish jumping, and he said the voice we heard must have been a sheep baaing, or maybe a night bird calling."

"That makes sense." I crossed my fingers, willing Davy to keep his mouth zipped.

"You should have seen us." Mom laughed again. "We insisted that the guide land on the island and we searched all over in the dark."

Our stuff! I'd forgotten we'd left all our beach things behind. "Did you find anything?" I asked, so tense I could hardly breathe.

"Yes, a couple of bags and some banana skins."

I stopped breathing.

"But just as all of us mothers began to go a little crazy, a young man—I think he was British—arrived on a powerboat and explained that the things were his. He was planning to camp out on the island overnight."

My knees went weak with relief. Thank goodness for Stephen!

"He also assured us there weren't any children on the island calling for their mommy. Well, we all felt a little foolish then and decided to continue the cruise." Mom chuckled. "But I noticed that as soon as we got back, all the parents headed for the phone, just to check and make sure things were okay at home."

"We're fine here!" I said quickly.

"I'm glad," Mom said. "I keep thinking of you both. There are a couple of kids down here—they seem to be brother and sister—and they look *amazingly* like you and Davy. I've only seen them briefly from a distance, but isn't that a coincidence?"

"Uh, yeah, it sure is," I said.

"Anyway," Mom said. "How are things in Connecticut?"

"Okay," I said. "It snowed."

"Is Miss Cuddy taking good care of you?"

"Well, she's a pretty good cook—"

Davy burst out, "She's mean! When are you coming home?"

"Oh dear. Don't worry, Davy, we'll be back soon. Try to be good and stay out of trouble."

"How's your vacation, Mom?" I asked, to be polite.

"It's wonderful! This is a beautiful island."

"We know," Davy said on the extension. "It's super!"

I wanted to strangle Davy, but he was out of reach in the other room. I said quickly, "He means we've been looking at the travel folder and the other stuff you left about Miracle—I mean, Mirabelle—Island."

"I see. Well, this call is costing a fortune! Good night. I miss you both. We'll see you Wednesday."

" 'Night, Mom."

"Come home soon!" Davy ordered.

"Okay, honey, as soon as we can."

I hung up and was about to go upstairs when Miss Cuddy swept into the kitchen, dragging Davy with her. "Jennifer, would you please put David to bed! Just look at him! He's quite flushed all over." She pulled up Davy's shirt, showing a reddish tan. "He's coming down with measles or whooping cough, or something dreadful, and I refuse to be exposed to him!"

She went back to the TV and I took Davy up to bed. As soon as we were alone, he said, "I was good, wasn't I? I didn't tell Mommy nothing, did I?"

I found his pajamas and helped him take off his shirt. "Well, almost nothing." I kept my voice very serious so he'd know I meant what I said. "But you *promised*—cross-your-heart-and-hope-to-die—that you wouldn't say a word."

"Yeah." He wouldn't look at me.

"I know it's hard, but Davy, you *can't* tell." I pulled his pajamas on and buttoned them up. "If you do, the magic will go away, and then we won't be able to take any more trips."

His eyes got big. "Never?"

"Never."

He thought about it. "Okay, cross-my-heart-and-hope-to-die-I-won't-tell." He hopped into bed and snuggled under the covers. "Can we go back tomorrow?"

"Maybe not tomorrow, but soon."

"When?" He yawned.

"You'll find out, *if* you keep your promise." I turned out the light and opened the door.

"I won't tell." He yawned again. "And Jenny?"

"Yes?"

"Thanks for taking me to Miracle."

"You're welcome."

I went to bed, thinking of London and Stephen. Would the experiment work? Tuesday seemed a zillion centuries away.

chapter sixteen

I was waiting on Carly's front steps, the new travel folder clutched to my chest, when she came home from swim practice Monday afternoon.

"I knew it," she said. "You can't wait until tomorrow, right?"

"I can't wait one more *second.* I just *have* to know if I can go to London."

There were still parts of Ophelia's letter I didn't understand, especially the business about "Nancy" or "Candy," but at least I was sure I had a real "exigency" to see if this experiment worked.

Carly looked me over. "You're all dressed up."

I'd spent an hour deciding on my blue skirt and sweater. "Just in case it works."

"You look terrific." She tilted her head, studying me. "You know, there's something different about you. You've changed."

"How?" I asked.

"I'm not sure. Something inside, like you're . . . stronger . . . kind of"—she searched for a word—"blooming."

"Really?" I'd have to think about that later. Right now our experiment was more important than anything else. "Please, Carly, let us in the house. I've got to find out if I can go to London."

She put her key in the lock. "Stephen probably isn't home yet. Wouldn't you rather wait?"

"Carly! I can't!"

"Okay, okay!" She opened the door. "Mom and Dad won't be back until six, so we have a little while. Want a snack first?"

"No!"

She held up her hands, grinning. "All *right,* take it easy."

I led her down the hall to her room. My knees were wobbling, my heart was racing, and it was hard to breathe.

Carly closed and locked her bedroom door. "Which picture are you going to use?"

I opened the new travel folder. "I'm not sure. Where would be the best place for me to show up? *If* I do?"

We studied the pictures. "Not Buckingham Palace," she said. "One of those guards might arrest you."

"How about here?" I pointed to a picture whose caption read: *Piccadilly Circus, the heart of London.* It didn't look anything like a circus; it was just a bustling, neon-lit city intersection.

"It looks kind of busy," Carly said. "Too many people might see you appear."

"But that might be safer. No one notices people in crowds." Also, the picture was taken at night, so I was pretty sure that's when I'd arrive, "when and where the medium dictates." It probably was a good idea to pop up in London after dark. "Besides, there should be pay phones around there, so I can call Stephen."

"Oh wow, you're going to need English money. I didn't think of that."

"I did." I was proud of myself. "I stopped at a bank near the travel agency. I have plenty of these weird-looking coins." I held out a handful.

"Good for you. Which one do you use in pay phones?"

"I don't know. I'll keep trying them until one works."

"Guess you're all set, then." She sat down on her bed. "Don't look so scared. You probably won't go to London after all."

"That's what I'm scared of!"

"Okay then, you probably *will* go." She grinned. "How long do you want to stay? When shall I call you back?"

"Miss Cuddy will be mad if I'm not home for dinner, so you'd better call me at five-thirty."

"Right. Well, okay, here we go."

I took a deep breath and stared at the picture of Piccadilly Circus. Playing with my ring, I concentrated hard, focusing on the sidewalk.

* * *

Car horns and traffic roars filled my ears. I smelled exhaust fumes. I opened my eyes as a red double-decker bus rolled past. It was evening; lights reflected off the damp pavement. People walked around me, most of them carrying umbrellas. I stood still on the sidewalk, blinking, and felt the most incredible joy.

I was in London! It had really happened! My wonderful, fantastic, crazy ring had done it again!

I couldn't wait to call Stephen, but I didn't see a phone booth. A nice lady pointed out something she called a kiosk. Sure enough, there was a phone inside. Hands shaking, I dropped coins in the slot, then discovered you only put the money in afterward. Finally I figured it out and a familiar voice answered.

"Stephen, it's me! Jenny!"

"Jenny! Where are you?" He sounded astonished.

"At a place called Piccadilly Circus."

"Do you mean it? You're here? In London?"

I nodded, even though he couldn't see me. "Yes, I'm here. I'm really, really here!"

"That's—that's marvelous! I can't believe it! I've only been home a few hours and I'm already talking to you. So your magical flights aren't limited to Mirabelle, are they? You *can* travel elsewhere!"

"Isn't it fantastic?" I looked around at the red buses, the beetle-shaped taxicabs, the lights, the crowds of people. Yes, I was actually here. "How do I find your house, Stephen?"

"I'll find you. Stand right in front of the statue. I'll

be there in fifteen minutes."

I walked over to the statue and stood still, breathing in the sights and sounds and smells of London while waves of excitement washed over me. If I could come here, with a little planning, I could go anywhere.

I smiled. "Get ready, world, here I come!"

Dear *Anywhere* Readers Everywhere,

Miracles can happen no matter who you are, where you live, or what your great-grandmother gives you for your birthday. With your imagination you can travel along with Jenny and explore the world together.

The Anywhere Ring will take you and Jenny to places—and times—you never dreamed of visiting. At least two hints of the future are hidden in Great-grandmother Ophelia's letter. Can you guess what they are?

And don't forget, Jenny still doesn't know all the secrets of the ring. Plus, crafty Ophelia has kept a few surprises to herself. Many of the delights—and frights—are yet to be discovered.

Jenny finds plenty of both in the next book, *Castle in Time*, in which she also discovers that

Stephen, even though he's a member of the male species, can be a good friend—and more—when life turns a little too fantastic.

The trouble begins when Stephen's sister Margaret disappears, and Stephen asks Jenny to take him to the wild Irish mountains to search for her. Without warning, they find themselves in an even wilder place and time: 16th century Ireland!

Jenny and Stephen are captured and taken to the McSheehy castle, where the king and his family recognize Jenny's magical powers and proclaim her a witch-queen. She discovers that being a witch and a queen can be exciting, especially when she learns the secret of the lost family treasure. But it turns terrifying when the powerful king decides to use Jenny's magic for his own purposes . . .

Hope to see you in Ireland soon!

Louise Ladd